Paul and Virginia

Bernardin de Saint Pierre

Contents

PAUL AND VIRGINIA

BY

Bernardin de Saint Pierre

PREFACE

In introducing to the Public the present edition of this well known and affecting Tale,--the *chef d'oeuvre* of its gifted author, the Publishers take occasion to say, that it affords them no little gratification, to apprise the numerous admirers of "Paul and Virginia," that the ***entire*** work of St. Pierre is now presented to them. All the previous editions have been disfigured by interpolations, and mutilated by numerous omissions and alterations, which have had the effect of reducing it from the rank of a Philosophical Tale, to the level of a mere story for children.

Of the merits of "Paul and Virginia," it is hardly necessary to utter a word; it tells its own story eloquently and impressively, and in a language simple, natural and true, it touches the common heart of the world. There are but few works that have obtained a greater degree of popularity, none are more deserving it; and the Publishers cannot therefore refrain from expressing a hope that their efforts in thus giving a faithful transcript of the work,--an acknowledged classic by the European world,--may be, in some degree, instrumental in awakening here, at home, a taste for those higher works of Fancy, which, while they seek to elevate and strengthen the understanding, instruct and purify the heart. It is in this character that the Tale of "Paul and Virginia" ranks pre-eminent. [Prepared from an edition published by Porter & Coates, Philadelphia, U.S.A.]

MEMOIR OF BERNARDIN DE ST. PIERRE

L ove of Nature, that strong feeling of enthusiasm which leads to profound admiration of the whole works of creation, belongs, it may be presumed, to a certain peculiarity of organization, and has, no doubt, existed in different individuals from the beginning of the world. The old poets and philosophers, romance writers, and troubadours, had all looked upon Nature with observing and admiring eyes. They have most of them given incidentally charming pictures of spring, of the setting sun, of particular spots, and of favourite flowers.

There are few writers of note, of any country, or of any age, from whom quotations might not be made in proof of the love with which they regarded Nature. And this remark applies as much to religious and philosophic writers as to poets,--equally to Plato, St. Francois de Sales, Bacon, and Fenelon, as to Shakespeare, Racine, Calderon, or Burns; for from no really philosophic or religious doctrine can the love of the works of Nature be excluded.

But before the days of Jean Jacques Rousseau, Buffon, and Bernardin de St. Pierre, this love of Nature had not been expressed in all its intensity. Until their day, it had not been written on exclusively. The lovers of Nature were not, till then, as they may perhaps since be considered, a sect apart. Though perfectly sincere in all the adorations they offered, they were less entirely, and certainly less diligently and constantly, her adorers.

It is the great praise of Bernardin de St. Pierre, that coming immediately after Rousseau and Buffon, and being one of the most proficient writers of the same school, he was in no degree their imitator, but perfectly original and new. He intuitively perceived the immensity of the subject he intended to explore, and has told us that no day of his life passed without his collecting some valuable materials for his writings. In the divine works of Nature, he diligently sought to discover her laws. It was his early intention not to begin to write until he had ceased to observe; but he found observation endless, and that he was "like a child who with a shell digs a hole in the sand to receive the waters of the ocean." He elsewhere humbly says, that not only the general history of Nature, but even that of the smallest plant, was far beyond his ability. Before, however, speaking further of him as an author, it will be necessary to recapitulate the chief events of his life.

HENRI-JACQUES BERNARDIN DE ST. PIERRE, was born at Havre in 1737. He always considered himself descended from that Eustache de St. Pierre, who is said by Froissart, (and I believe by Froissart only), to have so generously offered himself as a victim to appease the wrath of Edward the Third against Calais. He, with his companions in virtue, it is also said, was saved by the intercession of Queen Philippa. In one of his smaller works, Bernardin asserts this descent, and it was certainly one of which he might be proud. Many anecdotes are related of his childhood, indicative of the youthful author,--of his strong love of Nature, and his humanity to animals.

That "the child is the father of the man," has been seldom more strongly illustrated. There is a story of a cat, which, when related by him many years afterwards to Rousseau, caused that philosopher to shed tears. At eight years of age, he took the greatest pleasure in the regular culture of his garden; and possibly then stored up some of the ideas which afterwards appeared in the "Fraisier." His sympathy with all living things was extreme.

In "Paul and Virginia," he praises, with evident satisfaction, their meal of milk and eggs, which had not cost any animal its life. It has been remarked, and possibly with truth, that every tenderly disposed heart, deeply imbued with a love of Nature, is at times somewhat Braminical. St. Pierre's certainly was.

When quite young, he advanced with a clenched fist towards a carter who was ill-treating a horse. And when taken for the first time, by his father, to Rouen, having the towers of the cathedral pointed out to him, he exclaimed, "My God! how high they fly." Every one present naturally laughed. Bernardin had only noticed the flight of some swallows who had built their nests there. He thus early revealed those instincts which afterwards became the guidance of his life: the strength of which possibly occasioned his too great indifference to all monuments of art. The love of study and of solitude were also characteristics of his childhood. His temper is said to have been moody, impetuous, and intractable. Whether this faulty temper may not have been produced or rendered worse by mismanagement, cannot not be ascertained. It, undoubtedly became afterwards, to St. Pierre a fruitful source of misfortune and of woe.

The reading of voyages was with him, even in childhood, almost a passion. At twelve years of age, his whole soul was occupied by Robinson Crusoe and his island. His romantic love of adventure seeming to his parents to announce a predilection in favour of the sea, he was sent by them with one of his uncles to Martinique. But St. Pierre had not sufficiently practised the virtue of obedience to submit, as was necessary, to the discipline of a ship. He was afterwards placed with the Jesuits at Caen, with whom he made immense progress in his studies. But, it is to be feared, he did not conform too well to the regulations of the college, for he conceived, from that time, the greatest detestation for places of public education. And this aversion he has frequently testified in his writings. While devoted to his books of travels, he in turn anticipated being a Jesuit, a missionary or a martyr; but his family at length succeeded in establishing him at Rouen, where he completed his studies with brilliant success, in 1757. He soon after obtained a commission as an engineer, with a salary of one hundred louis. In this capacity he was sent (1760) to Dusseldorf, under the command of Count St. Germain. This was a career in which he might have acquired both honour and fortune; but, most unhappily for St. Pierre, he looked upon the useful and necessary etiquettes of life as so many unworthy prejudices. Instead of conforming to them, he sought to trample on them. In addition, he evinced some disposition to rebel against his commander, and was unsocial with his equals. It is not, therefore, to be wondered at, that at this unfortunate period of his existence, he made himself enemies; or that, notwithstanding his great talents, or the coolness he had exhibited in moments of danger, he should have been sent back to France. Unwelcome, under these circumstances, to his family, he was ill received by all.

It is a lesson yet to be learned, that genius gives no charter for the indulgence of error,--a truth yet *to be* remembered, that only a small portion of the world will look with leniency on the failings of the highly-gifted; and, that from themselves, the consequences of their own actions can never be averted. It is yet, alas! *to be* added to the convictions of the ardent in mind, that no degree of excellence in science or literature, not even the immortality of a name can exempt its possessor from obedience to moral discipline; or give him happiness, unless "temper's image" be stamped on his daily words and actions. St. Pierre's life was sadly embittered by his own conduct. The adventurous life he led after his return from Dusseldorf, some of the circumstances of which exhibited him in an unfavourable light to others, tended, perhaps, to tinge his imagination with that wild and tender melancholy so prevalent in his writings. A prize in the lottery had just doubled his very slender means of existence, when he obtained the appointment of geographical engineer, and was sent to Malta. The Knights of the Order were at this time expecting to be attacked by the Turks. Having already been in the service, it was singular that St. Pierre should have had the imprudence to sail without his commission. He thus subjected himself to a thousand disagreeables, for the officers would not recognize him as one of themselves. The effects of their neglect on his mind were tremendous; his reason for a time seemed almost disturbed by the mortifications he suffered. After receiving an insufficient indemnity for the expenses of his voyage, St. Pierre returned to France, there to endure fresh misfortunes.

Not being able to obtain any assistance from the ministry or his family, he resolved on giving lessons in the mathematics. But St. Pierre was less adapted than most others for succeeding in the apparently easy, but really ingenious and difficult, art of teaching. When education is better understood, it will be more generally acknowledged, that, to impart instruction with success, a teacher must possess deeper intelligence than is implied by the profoundest skill in any one branch of science or of art. All minds, even to the youngest, require, while being taught, the utmost compliance and consideration; and these qualities can scarcely be properly exercised without a true knowledge of the human heart, united to much practical patience. St. Pierre, at this period of his life, certainly did not possess them. It is probable that Rousseau, when he attempted in his youth to give lessons in music, not knowing any thing whatever of music, was scarcely less fitted for the task of instruction, than St. Pierre with all his mathematical knowledge. The pressure of poverty drove him to Holland. He was well received at Amsterdam, by a French refugee named Mustel, who edited a popular journal there, and who procured him employment, with handsome remuneration. St. Pierre did not, however, remain long satisfied with this quiet mode of existence. Allured by the encouraging reception given by Catherine II. to foreigners, he set out for St. Petersburg. Here, until he obtained the protection of the Marechal de Munich, and the friendship of Duval, he had again to contend with poverty. The latter generously opened to him his purse and by the Marechal he was introduced to Villebois, the Grand Master of Artillery, and by him presented to the Empress. St. Pierre was so handsome, that by some of his friends it was supposed, perhaps, too, hoped, that he would supersede Orloff in the favor of Catherine. But more honourable illusions, though they were but illusions, occupied his own mind. He neither sought nor wished to captivate the Empress. His ambition was to establish a republic on the shores of the lake Aral, of which in imitation of Plato or Rousseau, he was to be the legislator. Pre-occupied with the reformation of despotism, he did not sufficiently look into his own heart, or seek to avoid a repetition of the same errors that had already changed friends into enemies, and been such a terrible barrier to his success in life. His mind was already morbid, and in fancying that others did not understand him, he forgot that he did not understand others. The Empress, with the rank of captain, bestowed on him a grant of fifteen hundred francs; but when General Dubosquet proposed to take him with him to examine the military position of Finland, his only anxiety seemed to be to return to France: still he went to Finland; and his own notes of his occupations and experiments on that expedition prove, that he gave himself up in all diligence to considerations of attack and defence. He, who loved Nature so intently, seems only to have seen in the extensive and majestic forests of the north, a theatre of war. In this instance, he appears to have stifled every emotion of admiration, and to have beheld, alike, cities and countries in his character of military surveyor.

On his return to St. Petersburg, he found his protector Villebois, disgraced. St. Pierre then resolved on espousing the cause of the Poles. He went into Poland with a high reputation,--that of having refused the favours of despotism, to aid the cause of liberty. But it was his private life, rather than his public career, that was affected by his residence in Poland. The Princess Mary fell in love with him, and, forgetful of all considerations, quitted her family to reside with him. Yielding, however, at length, to the entreaties of her mother, she returned to her home. St. Pierre, filled with regret, resorted to Vienna; but, unable to support the sadness which oppressed him, and imagining that sadness to be shared by the Princess, he soon went back to Poland. His return was still more sad than his departure; for he found himself regarded by her who had once loved him, as an intruder. It is to this attachment he alludes so touchingly in one of his letters. "Adieu! friends dearer than the treasures of India! Adieu! forests of the North, that I shall never see again!--tender friendship, and the still dearer sentiment which surpassed it!--days of intoxication and of happiness adeiu! adieu! We live but for a day, to die during a whole life!"

This letter appears to one of St. Pierre's most partial biographers, as if steeped in tears; and he speaks of his romantic and unfortunate adventure in Poland, as the ideal of a poet's love.

"To be," says M. Sainte-Beuve, "a great poet, and loved before he had thought of glory! To exhale the first perfume of a soul of genius, believing himself only a lover! To reveal himself, for the first time, entirely, but in mystery!"

In his enthusiasm, M. Sainte-Beuve loses sight of the melancholy sequel, which must have left so sad a remembrance in St. Pierre's own mind. His suffering, from this circumstance, may perhaps have conduced to his making Virginia so good and true, and so incapable of giving pain.

In 1766, he returned to Havre; but his relations were by this time dead or dispersed, and after six years of exile, he found himself once more in his own country, without employment and destitute of pecuniary resources.

The Baron de Breteuil at length obtained for him a commission as Engineer to the Isle of France, whence he returned in 1771. In this interval, his heart and imagination doubtless received the germs of his immortal works. Many of the events, indeed, of the "Voyage a l'Ile de France," are to be found modified by imagined circumstances in "Paul and Virginia." He returned to Paris poor in purse, but rich in observation and mental resources, and resolved to devote himself to literature. By the Baron de Breteuil he was recommended to D'Alembert, who procured a publisher for his "Voyage," and also introduced him to Mlle. de l'Espinasse. But no one, in spite of his great beauty, was so ill calculated to shine or please in society as St. Pierre. His manners were timid and embarrassed, and, unless to those with whom he was very intimate, he scarcely appeared intelligent.

It is sad to think, that misunderstanding should prevail to such an extent, and heart so seldom really speak to heart, in the intercourse of the world, that the most humane may appear cruel, and the sympathizing indifferent. Judging of Mlle. de l'Espinasse from her letters, and the testimony of her contemporaries, it seems quite impossible that she could have given pain to any one, more particularly to a man possessing St. Pierre's extraordinary talent and profound sensibility. Both she and D'Alembert were capable of appreciating him; but the society in which they moved laughed at his timidity, and the tone of raillery in which they often indulged was not understood by him. It is certain that he withdrew from their circle with wounded and mortified feelings, and, in spite of an explanatory letter from D'Alembert, did not return to it. The inflictors of all this pain, in the meantime, were possibly as unconscious of the meaning attached to their words, as were the birds of old of the augury drawn from their flight.

St. Pierre, in his "Preambule de l'Arcadie," has pathetically and eloquently described the deplorable state of his health and feelings, after frequent humiliating disputes and disappointments had driven him from society; or rather, when, like Rousseau, he was "self-banished" from it.

"I was struck," he says, "with an extraordinary malady. Streams of fire, like lightning, flashed before my eyes; every object appeared to me double, or in motion: like OEdipus, I saw two suns. . . In the finest day of summer, I could not cross the Seine in a boat without experiencing intolerable anxiety. If, in a public garden, I merely passed by a piece of water, I suffered from spasms and a feeling of horror. I could not cross a garden in which many people were collected: if they looked at me, I immediately imagined they were speaking ill of me." It was during this state of suffering, that he devoted himself with ardour to collecting and making use of materials for that work which was to give glory to his name.

It was only by perseverance, and disregarding many rough and discouraging receptions, that he succeeded in making acquaintance with Rousseau, whom he so much resembled. St. Pierre devoted himself to his society with enthusiasm, visiting him frequently and constantly, till Rousseau departed for Ermenonville. It is not unworthy of remark, that both these men, such enthusiastic admirers of Nature and the natural in all things, should have possessed factitious rather than practical virtue, and a wisdom wholly unfitted for the world. St. Pierre asked Rousseau, in one of their frequent rambles, if, in delineating St. Preux, he had not intended to represent himself. "No," replied Rousseau, "St. Preux is not what I have been, but what I wished to be." St. Pierre would most likely have given the same answer, had a similar question been put to him with regard to the Colonel in "Paul and Virginia." This at least, appears the sort of old age he loved to contemplate, and wished to realize.

For six years, he worked at his "Etudes," and with some difficulty found a publisher for them. M. Didot, a celebrated typographer, whose daughter St. Pierre afterwards married, consented to print a manuscript which had been declined by many others. He was well rewarded for the undertaking. The success of the "Etudes de la Nature" surpassed the most sanguine expectation, even of the author. Four years after its publication, St. Pierre gave to the world "Paul and Virginia," which had for some time been lying in his portfolio. He had tried its effect, in manuscript, on persons of different characters and pursuits. They had given it no applause; but all had shed tears at its perusal: and perhaps, few works of a decidedly romantic character have ever been so generally read, or so much approved. Among the great names whose admiration of it is on record, may be mentioned Napoleon and Humboldt.

In 1789, he published "Les Veoeux d'un Solitaire," and "La Suite des Voeux." By the *Moniteur* of the day, these works were compared to the celebrated pamphlet of Sieyes,--"Qu'est-ce que le tiers etat?" which then absorbed all the public favour. In 1791, "La Chaumiere Indienne" was published: and in the following year, about thirteen days before the celebrated 10th of August, Louis XVI. appointed St. Pierre superintendant of the "Jardin des Plantes." Soon afterwards, the King, on seeing him, complimented him on his writings and told him he was happy to have found a worthy successor to Buffon.

Although deficient in the exact knowledge of the sciences, and knowing little of the world, St. Pierre was, by his simplicity, and the retirement in which he lived, well suited, at that epoch, to the situation. About this time, and when in his fifty-seventh year, he married Mlle. Didot.

In 1795, he became a member of the French Academy, and, as was just, after his acceptance of this honour, he wrote no more against literary societies. On the suppression of his place, he retired to Essonne. It is delightful to follow him there, and to contemplate his quiet existence. His days flowed on peaceably, occupied in the publication of "Les Harmonies de la Nature," the republication of his earlier works, and the composition of some lesser pieces. He himself affectingly regrets an interruption to these occupations. On being appointed Instructor to the Normal School, he says, "I am obliged to hang my harp on the willows of my river, and to accept an employment useful to my family and my country. I am afflicted at having to suspend an occupation which has given me so much happiness."

He enjoyed in his old age, a degree of opulence, which, as much as glory, had perhaps been the object of his ambition. In any case, it is gratifying to reflect, that after a life so full of chance and change, he was, in his latter years, surrounded by much that should accompany old age. His day of storms and tempests was closed by an evening of repose and beauty.

Amid many other blessings, the elasticity of his mind was preserved to the last. He died at Eragny sur l'Oise, on the 21st of January, 1814. The stirring events which then occupied France, or rather the whole world, caused his death to be little noticed at the time. The Academy did not, however, neglect to give him the honour due to its members. Mons. Parseval Grand Maison pronounced a deserved eulogium on his talents, and Mons. Aignan, also, the customary tribute, taking his seat as his successor.

Having himself contracted the habit of confiding his griefs and sorrows to the public, the sanctuary of his private life was open alike to the discussion of friends and enemies. The biographer, who wishes to be exact, and yet set down nought in malice, is forced to the contemplation of his errors. The secret of many of these, as well as of his miseries, seems revealed by himself in this sentence: "I experience more pain from a single thorn, than pleasure from a thousand roses." And elsewhere, "The best society seems to me bad, if I find in it one troublesome, wicked, slanderous, envious, or perfidious person." Now, taking into consideration that St. Pierre sometimes imagined persons who were really good, to be deserving of these strong and very contumacious epithets, it would have been difficult indeed to find a society in which he could have been happy. He was, therefore, wise, in seeking retirement, and indulging in solitude. His mistakes,--for they were mistakes,--arose from a too quick perception of evil, united to an exquisite and diffuse sensibility. When he felt wounded by a thorn, he forgot the beauty and perfume of the rose to which it belonged, and from which perhaps it could not be separated. And he was exposed (as often happens) to the very description of trials that were least in harmony with his defects. Few dispositions could have run a career like his, and have remained unscathed. But one less tender than his own would have been less soured by it. For many years, he bore about with him the consciousness of unacknowledged talent. The world cannot be blamed for not appreciating that which had never been revealed. But we know not what the jostling and elbowing of that world, in the meantime, may have been to him--how often he may have felt himself unworthily treated--or how far that treatment may have preyed upon and corroded his heart. Who shall say that with this consciousness there did not mingle a quick and instinctive perception of the hidden motives of action,--that he did not sometimes detect, where others might have been blind, the under-shuffling of the hands, in the by-play of the world?

Through all his writings, and throughout his correspondence, there are beautiful proofs of the tenderness of his feelings,--the most essential quality, perhaps, in any writer. It is at least, one that if not possessed, can never be attained. The familiarity of his imagination with natural objects, when he was living far removed from them, is remarkable, and often affecting.

"I have arranged," he says to Mr. Henin, his friend and patron, "very interesting materials, but it is only with the light of Heaven over me that I can recover my strength. Obtain for me a *rabbit's hole*, in which I may pass the summer in the country." And again, "With the *first violet*, I shall come to see you." It is soothing to find, in passages like these, such pleasing and convincing evidence that

"Nature never did betray,
The heart that loved her."

In the noise of a great city, in the midst of annoyances of many kinds these images, impressed with quietness and beauty, came back to the mind of St. Pierre, to cheer and animate him.

In alluding to his miseries, it is but fair to quote a passage from his "Voyage," which reveals his fond remembrance of his native land. "I should ever prefer my own country to every other," he says, "not because it was more beautiful, but because I was brought up in it. Happy he, who sees again the places where all was loved, and all was lovely!--the meadows in which he played, and the orchard that he robbed!"

He returned to this country, so fondly loved and deeply cherished in absence, to experience only trouble and difficulty. Away from it, he had yearned to behold it,--to fold it, as it were, once more to his bosom. He returned to feel as if neglected by it, and all his rapturous emotions were changed to bitterness and gall. His hopes had proved delusions--his expectations, mockeries. Oh! who but must look with charity and mercy on all discontent and irritation consequent on such a depth of disappointment: on what must have then appeared to him such unmitigable woe. Under the influence of these saddened feelings, his thoughts flew back to the island he had left, to place all beauty, as well as all happiness, there!

One great proof that he did beautify the distant, may be found in the contrast of some of the descriptions in the "Voyage a l'Ile de France," and those in "Paul and Virginia." That spot, which when peopled by the cherished creatures of his imagination, he described as an enchanting and delightful Eden, he had previously spoken of as a "rugged country covered with rocks,"--"a land of Cyclops blackened by fire." Truth, probably, lies between the two representations; the sadness of exile having darkened the one, and the exuberance of his imagination embellished the other.

St. Pierre's merit as an author has been too long and too universally acknowledged, to make it needful that it should be dwelt on here. A careful review of the circumstances of his life induces the belief, that his writings grew (if it may be permitted so to speak) out of his life. In his most imaginative passages, to whatever height his fancy soared, the starting point seems ever from a fact. The past appears to have been always spread out before him when he wrote, like a beautiful landscape, on which his eye rested with complacency, and from which his mind transferred and idealized some objects, without a servile imitation of any. When at Berlin, he had had it in his power to marry Virginia Tabenheim; and in Russia, Mlle. de la Tour, the niece of General Dubosquet, would have accepted his hand. He was too poor to marry either. A grateful recollection caused him to bestow the names of the two on his most beloved creation. Paul was the name of a friar, with whom he had associated in his childhood, and whose life he wished to imitate. How little had the owners of these names anticipated that they were to become the baptismal appellations of half a generation in France, and to be re-echoed through the world to the end of time!

It was St. Pierre who first discovered the poverty of language with regard to picturesque descriptions. In his earliest work, the often-quoted "Voyages," he complains, that the terms for describing nature are not yet invented. "Endeavour," he says, "to describe a mountain in such a manner that it may be recognised. When you have spoken of its base, its sides, its summit, you will have said all! But what variety there is to be found in those swelling, lengthened, flattened, or cavernous forms! It is only by periphrasis that all this can be expressed. The same difficulty exists for plains and valleys. But if you have a palace to describe, there is no longer any difficulty. Every moulding has its appropriate name."

It was St. Pierre's glory, in some degree, to triumph over this dearth of expression. Few authors ever introduced more new terms into descriptive writing: yet are his innovations ever chastened, and in good taste. His style, in its elegant simplicity, is, indeed, perfection. It is at once sonorous and sweet, and always in harmony with the sentiment he would express, or the subject he would discuss. Chenier might well arm himself with "Paul and Virginia," and the "Chaumiere Indienne," in opposition to those writers, who, as he said, made prose unnatural, by seeking to elevate it into verse.

The "Etudes de la Nature" embraced a thousand different subjects, and contained some new ideas on all. It is to the honour of human nature, that after the uptearing of so many sacred opinions, a production like this, revealing the chain of connection through the works of Creation, and the Creator in his works, should have been hailed, as it was, with enthusiasm.

His motto, from his favourite poet Virgil, "Taught by calamity, I pity the unhappy," won for him, perhaps many readers. And in its touching illusions, the unhappy may have found suspension from the realities of life, as well as encouragement to support its trials. For, throughout, it infuses admiration of the arrangements of Providence, and a desire for virtue. More than one modern poet may be supposed to have drawn a portion of his inspiration, from the "Etudes." As a work of science it contains many errors. These, particularly his theory of the tides,[1] St. Pierre maintained to the last, and so eloquently, that it was said at the time, to be impossible to unite less reason with more logic.

In "Paul and Virginia," he was supremely fortunate in his subject. It was an entirely new creation, uninspired by any previous work; but which gave birth to many others, having furnished the plot to six theatrical pieces. It was a subject to

1   Occasioned, according to St. Pierre, by the melting of the ice at the Poles.

which the author could bring all his excellences as a writer and a man, while his deficiencies and defects were necessarily excluded. In no manner could he incorporate politics, science, or misapprehension of persons, while his sensibility, morals, and wonderful talent for description, were in perfect accordance with, and ornaments to it. Lemontey and Sainte-Beuve both consider success to be inseparable from the happy selection of a story so entirely in harmony with the character of the author; and that the most successful writers might envy him so fortunate a choice. Buonaparte was in the habit of saying, whenever he saw St. Pierre, "M. Bernardin, when do you mean to give us more Pauls and Virginias, and Indian Cottages? You ought to give us some every six months."

The "Indian Cottage," if not quite equal in interest to "Paul and Virginia," is still a charming production, and does great honour to the genius of its author. It abounds in antique and Eastern gems of thought. Striking and excellent comparisons are scattered through its pages; and it is delightful to reflect, that the following beautiful and solemn answer of the Paria was, with St. Pierre, the results of his own experience:--"Misfortune resembles the Black Mountain of Bember, situated at the extremity of the burning kingdom of Lahore; while you are climbing it, you only see before you barren rocks; but when you have reached its summit, you see heaven above your head, and at your feet the kingdom of Cachemere."

When this passage was written, the rugged, and sterile rock had been climbed by its gifted author. He had reached the summit,--his genius had been rewarded, and he himself saw the heaven he wished to point out to others.

SARAH JONES.

[For the facts contained in this brief Memoir, I am indebted to St. Pierre's own works, to the "Biographie Universelle," to the "Essai sur la Vie et les Ouvrages de Bernardin de St. Pierre," by M. Aime Martin, and to the very excellent and interesting "Notice Historique et Litteraire," of M. Sainte-Beuve.]

PAUL AND VIRGINIA

Situated on the eastern side of the mountain which rises above Port Louis, in the Mauritius, upon a piece of land bearing the marks of former cultivation, are seen the ruins of two small cottages. These ruins are not far from the centre of a valley, formed by immense rocks, and which opens only towards the north. On the left rises the mountain called the Height of Discovery, whence the eye marks the distant sail when it first touches the verge of the horizon, and whence the signal is given when a vessel approaches the island. At the foot of this mountain stands the town of Port Louis. On the right is formed the road which stretches from Port Louis to the Shaddock Grove, where the church bearing that name lifts its head, surrounded by its avenues of bamboo, in the middle of a spacious plain; and the prospect terminates in a forest extending to the furthest bounds of the island. The front view presents the bay, denominated the Bay of the Tomb; a little on the right is seen the Cape of Misfortune; and beyond rolls the expanded ocean, on the surface of which appear a few uninhabited islands; and, among others, the Point of Endeavour, which resembles a bastion built upon the flood.

At the entrance of the valley which presents these various objects, the echoes of the mountain incessantly repeat the hollow murmurs of the winds that shake the neighbouring forests, and the tumultuous dashing of the waves which break at a distance upon the cliffs; but near the ruined cottages all is calm and still, and the only objects which there meet the eye are rude steep rocks, that rise like a surrounding rampart. Large clumps of trees grow at their base, on their rifted sides, and even on their majestic tops, where the clouds seem to repose. The showers, which their bold points attract, often paint the vivid colours of the rainbow on their green and brown declivities, and swell the sources of the little river which flows at their feet, called the river of Fan-Palms. Within this inclosure reigns the most profound silence. The waters, the air, all the elements are at peace. Scarcely does the echo repeat the whispers of the palm-trees spreading their broad leaves, the long points of which are gently agitated by the winds. A soft light illumines the bottom of this deep valley, on which the sun shines only at noon. But, even at the break of day, the rays of light are thrown on the surrounding rocks; and their sharp peaks, rising above the shadows of the mountain, appear like tints of gold and purple gleaming upon the azure sky.

To this scene I loved to resort, as I could here enjoy at once the richness of an unbounded landscape, and the charm of uninterrupted solitude. One day, when I was seated at the foot of the cottages, and contemplating their ruins, a man, advanced in years, passed near the spot. He was dressed in the ancient garb of the island, his feet were bare, and he leaned upon a staff of ebony; his hair was white, and the expression of his countenance was dignified and interesting. I bowed to him with respect; he returned the salutation; and, after looking at me with some earnestness, came and placed himself upon the hillock on which I was seated. Encouraged by this mark of confidence I thus addressed him: "Father, can you tell me to whom those cottages once belonged?"--"My son," replied the old man, "those heaps of rubbish, and that untilled land, were, twenty years ago, the property of two families, who then found happiness in this solitude. Their history is affecting; but what European, pursuing his way to the Indies, will pause one moment to interest himself in the fate of a few obscure individuals? What European can picture happiness to his imagination amidst poverty and neglect? The curiosity of mankind is only attracted by the history of the great, and yet from that knowledge little use can be derived."--"Father," I rejoined, "from your manner and your observations, I perceive that you have acquired much experience of human life. If you have leisure, relate to me, I beseech you, the history of the ancient inhabitants of this desert; and be assured, that even the men who are most perverted by the prejudices of the world, find a soothing pleasure in contemplating that happiness which belongs to simplicity and virtue." The old man, after a short silence, during which he leaned his face upon his hands, as if he were trying to recall the images of the past, thus began his narration:--

Monsieur de la Tour, a young man who was a native of Normandy, after having in vain solicited a commission in the French army, or some support from his own family, at length determined to seek his fortune in this island, where he arrived in 1726. He brought hither a young woman, whom he loved tenderly, and by whom he was no less tenderly beloved. She belonged to a rich and ancient family of the same province: but he had married her secretly and without fortune, and in opposition to the will of her relations, who refused their consent because he was found guilty of being descended from parents who had no claims to nobility. Monsieur de la Tour, leaving his wife at Port Louis, embarked for Madagascar, in order to purchase a few slaves, to assist him in forming a plantation on this island. He landed at Madagascar during that unhealthy season which commences about the middle of October; and soon after his arrival died of the pestilential fever, which prevails in that island six months of the year, and which will forever baffle the attempts of the European nations to form establishments on that fatal soil. His effects were seized upon by the rapacity of strangers, as commonly happens to persons dying in foreign parts; and his wife, who was pregnant, found herself a widow in a country where she had neither credit nor acquaintance, and no earthly possession, or rather support, but one negro woman. Too delicate to solicit protection or relief from any one else after the death of him whom alone she loved, misfortune armed her with courage, and she resolved to cultivate, with her slave, a little spot of ground, and procure for herself the means of subsistence.

Desert as was the island, and the ground left to the choice of the settler, she avoided those spots which were most fertile and most favorable to commerce: seeking some nook of the mountain, some secret asylum where she might live solitary and unknown, she bent her way from the town towards these rocks, where she might conceal herself from observation. All sensitive and suffering creatures, from a sort of common instinct, fly for refuge amidst their pains to haunts the most wild and desolate; as if rocks could form a rampart against misfortune--as if the calm of Nature could hush the tumults of the soul. That Providence, which lends its support when we ask but the supply of our necessary wants, had a blessing in reserve for Madame de la Tour, which neither riches nor greatness can purchase:--this blessing was a friend.

The spot to which Madame de la Tour had fled had already been inhabited for a year by a young woman of a lively, good-natured and affectionate disposition. Margaret (for that was her name) was born in Brittany, of a family of peasants, by whom she was cherished and beloved, and with whom she might have passed through life in simple rustic happiness, if, misled by the weakness of a tender heart, she had not listened to the passion of a gentleman in the neighbourhood, who promised her marriage. He soon abandoned her, and adding inhumanity to seduction, refused to insure a provision for the child of which she was pregnant. Margaret then determined to leave forever her native village, and retire, where her fault might be concealed, to some colony distant from that country where she had lost the only portion of a poor peasant girl--her reputation. With some borrowed money she purchased an old negro slave, with whom she cultivated a little corner of this district.

Madame de la Tour, followed by her negro woman, came to this spot, where she found Margaret engaged in suckling her child. Soothed and charmed by the sight of a person in a situation somewhat similar to her own, Madame de la Tour related, in a few words, her past condition and her present wants. Margaret was deeply affected by the recital; and more anxious to merit confidence than to create esteem, she confessed without disguise, the errors of which she had been guilty. "As for me," said she, "I deserve my fate: but you, madam--you! at once virtuous and unhappy"--and, sobbing, she offered Madame de la Tour both her hut and her friendship. That lady, affected by this tender reception, pressed her in her arms, and exclaimed,--"Ah surely Heaven has put an end to my misfortunes, since it inspires you, to whom I am a stranger, with more goodness towards me than I have ever experienced from my own relations!"

I was acquainted with Margaret: and, although my habitation is a league and a half from hence, in the woods behind that sloping mountain, I considered myself as her neighbour. In the cities of Europe, a street, even a simple wall, frequently prevents members of the same family from meeting for years; but in new colonies we consider those persons as neighbours from whom we are divided only by woods and mountains; and above all at that period, when this island had little intercourse with the Indies, vicinity alone gave a claim to friendship, and hospitality towards strangers seemed less a duty than a pleasure. No sooner was I informed that Margaret had found a companion, than I hastened to her, in the hope of being useful to my neighbour and her guest. I found Madame de la Tour possessed of all those melancholy graces which, by blending sympathy with admiration give to beauty additional power. Her countenance was interesting, expressive at once of dignity and dejection. She appeared to be in the last stage of her pregnancy. I told the two friends that for the future interests of their children, and to prevent the intrusion of any other settler, they had better divide between them the property of this wild, sequestered valley, which is nearly twenty acres in extent. They confided that task to me, and I marked out two equal portions of land. One included the higher part of this enclosure, from the cloudy pinnacle of that rock, whence springs the river of Fan-Palms, to that precipitous cleft which you see on the summit of the mountain, and which, from its resemblance in form to the battlement of a fortress, is called the Embrasure. It is difficult to find a path along this wild portion of the enclosure, the soil of which is encumbered with fragments of rock, or worn into channels formed by torrents; yet it produces noble trees, and innumerable springs and rivulets. The other portion of land comprised the plain extending along the banks of the river of Fan-Palms, to the opening where we are now seated, whence the river takes its course between these two hills, until it falls into the sea. You may still trace the vestiges of some meadow land; and this part of the common is less rugged, but not more valuable than the other; since in the rainy season it becomes marshy, and in dry weather is so hard and unyielding, that it will almost resist the stroke of the pickaxe. When I had thus divided the property, I persuaded my neighbours to draw lots for their respective possessions. The higher portion of land, containing the source of the river of Fan-Palms, became the property of Madame de la Tour; the lower, comprising the plain on the banks of the river, was allotted to Margaret; and each seemed satisfied with her share. They entreated me to place their habitations together, that they might at all times enjoy the soothing intercourse of friendship, and the consolation of mutual kind offices. Margaret's cottage was situated near the centre of the valley, and just on the boundary of her own plantation. Close to that spot I built another cottage for the residence of Madame de la Tour; and thus the two friends, while they possessed all the advantages of neighbourhood lived on their own property. I myself cut palisades from the mountain, and brought leaves of fan-palms from the sea-shore in order to construct those two cottages, of which you can now discern neither the entrance nor the roof. Yet, alas! there still remains but too many traces for my remembrance! Time, which so rapidly destroys the proud monuments of empires, seems in this desert to spare those of friendship, as if to perpetuate my regrets to the last hour of my existence.

As soon as the second cottage was finished, Madame de la Tour was delivered of a girl. I had been the godfather of Margaret's child, who was christened by the name of Paul. Madame de la Tour desired me to perform the same office for her child also, together with her friend, who gave her the name of Virginia. "She will be virtuous," cried Margaret, "and she will be happy. I have only known misfortune by wandering from virtue."

About the time Madame de la Tour recovered, these two little estates had already begun to yield some produce, perhaps in a small degree owing to the care which I occasionally bestowed on their improvement, but far more to the indefatigable labours of the two slaves. Margaret's slave, who was called Domingo, was still healthy and robust, though advanced in years: he possessed some knowledge, and a good natural understanding. He cultivated indiscriminately, on both plantations, the spots of ground that seemed most fertile, and sowed whatever grain he thought most congenial to each particular soil. Where the ground was poor, he strewed maize; where it was most fruitful, he planted wheat; and rice in such spots as were marshy. He threw the seeds of gourds and cucumbers at the foot of the rocks, which they loved to climb and decorate with their luxuriant foliage. In dry spots he cultivated the sweet potatoe; the cotton-tree flourished upon the heights, and the sugar-cane grew in the clayey soil. He reared some plants of coffee on the hills, where the grain, although small, is excellent. His plantain-trees, which spread their grateful shade on the banks of the river, and encircled the cottages, yielded fruit throughout the year. And lastly, Domingo, to soothe his cares, cultivated a few plants of tobacco. Sometimes he was employed in cutting wood for firing from the mountain, sometimes in hewing pieces of rock within the enclosure, in order to level the paths. The zeal which inspired him enabled him to perform all these labours with intelligence and activity. He was much attached to Margaret, and not less to Madame de la Tour, whose negro woman, Mary, he had married on the birth of Virginia; and he was passionately fond of his wife. Mary was born at Madagascar, and had there acquired the knowledge of some useful arts. She could weave baskets, and a sort of stuff, with long grass that grows in the woods. She was active, cleanly, and, above all, faithful. It was her care to prepare their meals, to rear the poultry, and go sometimes to Port Louis, to sell the superfluous produce of these little plantations, which was not however, very considerable. If you add to the personages already mentioned two goats, which were brought up with the children, and a great dog, which kept watch at night, you will have a complete idea of the household, as well as of the productions of these two little farms.

Madame de la Tour and her friend were constantly employed in spinning cotton for the use of their families. Destitute of everything which their own industry could not supply, at home they went bare-footed: shoes were a convenience reserved for Sunday, on which day, at an early hour, they attended mass at the church of the Shaddock Grove, which you see yonder. That church was more distant from their homes than Port Louis; but they seldom visited the town, lest they should be treated with contempt on account of their dress, which consisted simply of the coarse blue linen of Bengal, usually worn by slaves. But is there, in that external deference which fortune commands, a compensation for domestic happiness? If these interesting women had something to suffer from the world, their homes on that very account became more dear to them. No sooner did Mary and Domingo, from this elevated spot, perceive their mistresses on the road of the Shaddock Grove, than they flew to the foot of the mountain in order to help them to ascend. They discerned in the looks of their domestics the joy which their return excited. They found in their retreat neatness, independence, all the blessings which are the recompense of toil, and they received the zealous services which spring from affection. United by the tie of similar wants, and the sympathy of similar misfortunes, they gave each other the tender names of companion, friend, sister. They had but one will, one interest, one table. All their possessions were in common. And if sometimes a passion more ardent than friendship awakened in their hearts the pang of unavailing anguish, a pure religion, united with chaste manners, drew their affections towards another life: as the trembling flame rises towards heaven, when it no longer finds any ailment on earth.

The duties of maternity became a source of additional happiness to these affectionate mothers, whose mutual friendship gained new strength at the sight of their children, equally the offspring of an ill-fated attachment. They delighted in washing their infants together in the same bath, in putting them to rest in the same cradle, and in changing the maternal bosom at which they received nourishment. "My friend," cried Madame de la Tour, "we shall each of us have two children, and each of our children will have two mothers." As two buds which remain on different trees of the same kind, after the tempest has broken all their branches, produce more delicious fruit, if each, separated from the maternal stem, be grafted on the neighbouring tree, so these two infants, deprived of all their other relations, when thus exchanged for nourishment by those who had given them birth, imbibed feelings of affection still more tender than those of son and daughter, brother and sister. While they were yet in their cradles, their mothers talked of their marriage. They soothed their own cares by looking forward to the future happiness of their children; but this contemplation often drew forth their tears. The misfortunes of one mother had arisen from having neglected marriage; those of the other from having submitted to its laws. One had suffered by aiming to rise above her condition, the other by descending from her rank. But they found consolation in reflecting that their more fortunate children, far from the cruel prejudices of Europe, would enjoy at once the pleasures of love and the blessings of equality.

Rarely, indeed, has such an attachment been seen as that which the two children already testified for each other. If Paul complained of anything, his mother pointed to Virginia: at her sight he smiled, and was appeased. If any accident befel Virginia, the cries of Paul gave notice of the disaster; but the dear little creature would suppress her complaints if she found that he was unhappy. When I came hither, I usually found them quite naked, as is the custom of the country, tottering in their walk, and holding each other by the hands and under the arms, as we see represented in the constellation of the Twins. At night these infants often refused to be separated, and were found lying in the same cradle, their cheeks, their bosoms pressed close together, their hands thrown round each other's neck, and sleeping, locked in one another's arms.

When they first began to speak, the first name they learned to give each other were those of brother and sister, and childhood knows no softer appellation. Their education, by directing them ever to consider each other's wants, tended greatly to increase their affection. In a short time, all the household economy, the care of preparing their rural repasts, became the task of Virginia, whose labours were always crowned with the praises and kisses of her brother. As for Paul, always in motion, he dug the garden with Domingo, or followed him with a little hatchet into the woods; and if, in his rambles he espied a beautiful flower, any delicious fruit, or a nest of birds, even at the top of the tree, he would climb up and bring the spoil to his sister. When you met one of these children, you might be sure the other was not far off.

One day as I was coming down that mountain, I saw Virginia at the end of the garden running towards the house with her petticoat thrown over her head, in order to screen herself from a shower of rain. At a distance, I thought she was alone; but as I hastened towards her in order to help her on, I perceived she held Paul by the arm, almost entirely enveloped in the same canopy, and both were laughing heartily at their being sheltered together under an umbrella of their own invention. Those two charming faces in the middle of a swelling petticoat, recalled to my mind the children of Leda, enclosed in the same shell.

Their sole study was how they could please and assist one another; for of all other things they were ignorant, and indeed could neither read nor write. They were never disturbed by inquiries about past times, nor did their curiosity extend beyond the bounds of their mountain. They believed the world ended at the shores of their own island, and all their ideas and all their affections were confined within its limits. Their mutual tenderness, and that of their mothers, employed all the energies of their minds. Their tears had never been called forth by tedious application to useless sciences. Their minds had never been wearied by lessons of morality, superfluous to bosoms unconscious of ill. They had never been taught not to steal, because every thing with them was in common: or not to be intemperate, because their simple food was left to their own discretion; or not to lie, because they had nothing to conceal. Their young imaginations had never been terrified by the idea that God has punishment in store for ungrateful children, since, with them, filial affection arose naturally from maternal tenderness. All they had been taught of religion was to love it, and if they did not offer up long prayers in the church, wherever they were, in the house, in the fields, in the woods, they raised towards heaven their innocent hands, and hearts purified by virtuous affections.

All their early childhood passed thus, like a beautiful dawn, the prelude of a bright day. Already they assisted their mothers in the duties of the household. As soon as the crowing of the wakeful cock announced the first beam of the morning, Virginia arose, and hastened to draw water from a neighbouring spring: then returning to the house she prepared the breakfast. When the rising sun gilded the points of the rocks which overhang the enclosure in which they lived, Margaret and her child repaired to the dwelling of Madame de la Tour, where they offered up their morning prayer together. This sacrifice of thanksgiving always preceded their first repast, which they often took before the door of the cottage, seated upon the grass, under a canopy of plantain: and while the branches of that delicious tree afforded a grateful shade, its fruit furnished a substantial food ready prepared for them by nature, and its long glossy leaves, spread upon the table, supplied the place of linen. Plentiful and wholesome nourishment gave early growth and vigour to the persons of these children, and their countenances expressed the purity and the peace of their souls. At twelve years of age the figure of Virginia was in some degree formed: a profusion of light hair shaded her face, to which her blue eyes and coral lips gave the most charming brilliancy. Her eyes sparkled with vivacity when she spoke; but when she was silent they were habitually turned upwards, with an expression of extreme sensibility, or rather of tender melancholy. The figure of Paul began already to display the graces of youthful beauty. He was taller than Virginia: his skin was of a darker tint; his nose more aquiline; and his black eyes would have been too piercing, if the long eye-lashes by which they were shaded, had not imparted to them an expression of softness. He was constantly in motion, except when his sister appeared, and then, seated by her side, he became still. Their meals often passed without a word being spoken; and from their silence, the simple elegance of their attitudes, and the beauty of their naked feet, you might have fancied you beheld an antique group of white marble, representing some of the children of Niobe, but for the glances of their eyes, which were constantly seeking to meet, and their mutual soft and tender smiles, which suggested rather the idea of happy celestial spirits, whose nature is love, and who are not obliged to have recourse to words for the expression of their feelings.

In the meantime Madame de la Tour, perceiving every day some unfolding grace, some new beauty, in her daughter, felt her maternal anxiety increase with her tenderness. She often said to me, "If I were to die, what would become of Virginia without fortune?"

Madame de la Tour had an aunt in France, who was a woman of quality, rich, old, and a complete devotee. She had behaved with so much cruelty towards her niece upon her marriage, that Madame de la Tour had determined no extremity of distress should ever compel her to have recourse to her hard-hearted relation. But when she became a mother, the pride of resentment was overcome by the stronger feelings of maternal tenderness. She wrote to her aunt, informing her of the sudden death of her husband, the birth of her daughter, and the difficulties in which she was involved, burthened as she was with an infant, and without means of support. She received no answer; but notwithstanding the high spirit natural to her character, she no longer feared exposing herself to mortification; and, although she knew her aunt would never pardon her for having married a man who was not of noble birth, however estimable, she continued to write to her, with the hope of awakening her compassion for Virginia. Many years, however passed without receiving any token of her remembrance.

At length, in 1738, three years after the arrival of Monsieur de la Bourdonnais in this island, Madame de la Tour was informed that the Governor had a letter to give her from her aunt. She flew to Port Louis; maternal joy raised her mind above all trifling considerations, and she was careless on this occasion of appearing in her homely attire. Monsieur de la Bourdonnais gave her a letter from her aunt, in which she informed her, that she deserved her fate for marrying an adventurer and a libertine: that the passions brought with them their own punishment; that the premature death of her husband was a just visitation from Heaven; that she had done well in going to a distant island, rather than dishonour her family by remaining in France; and that, after all, in the colony where she had taken refuge, none but the idle failed to grow rich. Having thus censured her niece, she concluded by eulogizing herself. To avoid, she said, the almost inevitable evils of marriage, she had determined to remain single. In fact, as she was of a very ambitious disposition she had resolved to marry none but a man of high rank; but although she was very rich, her fortune was not found a sufficient bribe, even at court, to counterbalance the malignant dispositions of her mind, and the disagreeable qualities of her person.

After mature deliberations, she added, in a postscript, that she had strongly recommended her niece to Monsieur de la Bourdonnais. This she had indeed done, but in a manner of late too common which renders a patron perhaps even more to be feared than a declared enemy; for, in order to justify herself for her harshness, she had cruelly slandered her niece, while she affected to pity her misfortunes.

Madame de la Tour, whom no unprejudiced person could have seen without feelings of sympathy and respect, was received with the utmost coolness by Monsieur de la Bourdonnais, biased as he was against her. When she painted to him her own situation and that of her child, he replied in abrupt sentences,--"We shall see what can be done--there are so many to relieve--all in good time--why did you displease your aunt?--you have been much to blame."

Madame de la Tour returned to her cottage, her heart torn with grief, and filled with all the bitterness of disappointment. When she arrived, she threw her aunt's letter on the table, and exclaimed to her friend,--"There is the fruit of eleven years of patient expectation!" Madame de la Tour being the only person in the little circle who could read, she again took up the letter, and read it aloud. Scarcely had she finished, when Margaret exclaimed, "What have we to do with your relations? Has God then forsaken us? He only is our father! Have we not hitherto been happy? Why then this regret? You have no courage." Seeing Madame de la Tour in tears, she threw herself upon her neck, and pressing her in her arms,--"My dear friend!" cried she, "my dear friend!"--but her emotion choked her utterance. At this sight Virginia burst into tears, and pressed her mother's and Margaret's hand alternately to her lips and heart; while Paul, his eyes inflamed with anger, cried, clasped his hands together, and stamped his foot, not knowing whom to blame for this scene of misery. The noise soon brought Domingo and Mary to the spot, and the little habitation resounded with cries of distress,--"Ah, madame!--My good mistress!--My dear mother!--Do not weep!" These tender proofs of affections at length dispelled the grief of Madame de la Tour. She took Paul and Virginia in her arms, and, embracing them, said, "You are the cause of my affliction, my children, but you are also my only source of delight! Yes, my dear children, misfortune has reached me, but only from a distance: here, I am surrounded with happiness." Paul and Virginia did not understand this reflection; but, when they saw that she was calm, they smiled, and continued to caress her. Tranquillity was thus restored in this happy family, and all that had passed was but a storm in the midst of fine weather, which disturbs the serenity of the atmosphere but for a short time, and then passes away.

The amiable disposition of these children unfolded itself daily. One Sunday, at day-break, their mothers having gone to mass at the church of Shaddock Grove, the children perceived a negro woman beneath the plantains which surrounded their habitation. She appeared almost wasted to a skeleton, and had no other garment than a piece of coarse cloth thrown around her. She threw herself at the feet of Virginia, who was preparing the family breakfast, and said, "My good young lady, have pity on a poor runaway slave. For a whole month I have wandered among these mountains, half dead with hunger, and often pursued by the hunters and their dogs. I fled from my master, a rich planter of the Black River, who has used me as you see;" and she showed her body marked with scars from the lashes she had received. She added, "I was going to drown myself, but hearing you lived here, I said to myself, since there are still some good white people in this country, I need not die yet." Virginia answered with emotion,--"Take courage, unfortunate creature! here is something to eat;" and she gave her the breakfast she had been preparing, which the slave in a few minutes devoured. When her hunger was appeased, Virginia said to her,--"Poor woman! I should like to go and ask forgiveness for you of your master. Surely the sight of you will touch him with pity. Will you show me the way?"--"Angel of heaven!" answered the poor negro woman, "I will follow you where you please!" Virginia called her brother, and begged him to accompany her. The slave led the way, by winding and difficult paths, through the woods, over mountains, which they climbed with difficulty, and across rivers, through which they were obliged to wade. At length, about the middle of the day, they reached the foot of a steep descent upon the borders of the Black River. There they perceived a well-built house, surrounded by extensive plantations, and a number of slaves employed in their various labours. Their master was walking among them with a pipe in his mouth, and a switch in his hand. He was a tall thin man, of a brown complexion; his eyes were sunk in his head, and his dark eyebrows were joined in one. Virginia, holding Paul by the hand, drew near, and with much emotion begged him, for the love of God, to pardon his poor slave, who stood trembling a few paces behind. The planter at first paid little attention to the children, who, he saw, were meanly dressed. But when he observed the elegance of Virginia's form, and the profusion of her beautiful light tresses which had escaped from beneath her blue cap; when he heard the soft tone of her voice, which trembled, as well as her whole frame, while she implored his compassion; he took his pipe from his mouth, and lifting up his stick, swore, with a terrible oath, that he pardoned his slave, not for the love of Heaven, but of her who asked his forgiveness. Virginia made a sign to the slave to approach her master; and instantly sprang away followed by Paul.

They climbed up the steep they had descended; and having gained the summit, seated themselves at the foot of a tree, overcome with fatigue, hunger and thirst. They had left their home fasting, and walked five leagues since sunrise. Paul said to Virginia,--"My dear sister, it is past noon, and I am sure you are thirsty and hungry: we shall find no dinner here; let us go down the mountain again, and ask the master of the poor slave for some food."--"Oh, no," answered Virginia, "he frightens me too much. Remember what mamma sometimes says, 'The bread of the wicked is like stones in the mouth.' "--"What shall we do then," said Paul; "these trees produce no fruit fit to eat; and I shall not be able to find even a tamarind or a lemon to refresh you."--"God will take care of us," replied Virginia; "he listens to the cry even of the little birds when they ask him for food." Scarcely had she pronounced these words when they heard the noise of water falling from a neighbouring rock. They ran thither and having quenched their thirst at this crystal spring, they gathered and ate a few cresses which grew on the border of the stream. Soon afterwards while they were wandering backwards and forwards in search of more solid nourishment, Virginia perceived in the thickest part of the forest, a young palm-tree. The kind of cabbage which is found at the top of the palm, enfolded within its leaves, is well adapted for food; but, although the stock of the tree is not thicker than a man's leg, it grows to above sixty feet in height. The wood of the tree, indeed, is composed only of very fine filaments; but the bark is so hard that it turns the edge of the hatchet, and Paul was not furnished even with a knife. At length he thought of setting fire to the palm-tree; but a new difficulty occurred: he had no steel with which to strike fire; and although the whole island is covered with rocks, I do not believe it is possible to find a single flint. Necessity, however, is fertile in expedients, and the most useful inventions have arisen from men placed in the most destitute situations. Paul determined to kindle a fire after the manner of the negroes. With the sharp end of a stone he made a small hole in the branch of a tree that was quite dry, and which he held between his feet: he then, with the edge of the same stone, brought to a point another dry branch of a different sort of wood, and, afterwards, placing the piece of pointed wood in the small hole of the branch which he held with his feet and turning it rapidly between his hands, in a few minutes smoke and sparks of fire issued from the point of contact. Paul then heaped together dried grass and branches, and set fire to the foot of the palm-tree, which soon fell to the ground with a tremendous crash. The fire was further useful to him in stripping off the long, thick, and pointed leaves, within which the cabbage was inclosed. Having thus succeeded in obtaining this fruit, they ate part of it raw, and part dressed upon the ashes, which they found equally palatable. They made this frugal repast with delight, from the remembrances of the benevolent action they had performed in the morning: yet their joy was embittered by the thoughts of the uneasiness which their long absence from home would occasion their mothers. Virginia often recurred to this subject; but Paul, who felt his strength renewed by their meal, assured her, that it would not be long before they reached home, and, by the assurance of their safety, tranquillized the minds of their parents.

After dinner they were much embarrassed by the recollection that they had now no guide, and that they were ignorant of the way. Paul, whose spirit was not subdued by difficulties, said to Virginia,--"The sun shines full upon our huts at noon: we must pass, as we did this morning, over that mountain with its three points, which you see yonder. Come, let us be moving." This mountain was that of the Three Breasts, so called from the form of its three peaks. They then descended the steep bank of the Black River, on the northern side; and arrived, after an hour's walk, on the banks of a large river, which stopped their further progress. This large portion of the island, covered as it is with forests, is even now so little known that many of its rivers and mountains have not yet received a name. The stream, on the banks of which Paul and Virginia were now standing, rolls foaming over a bed of rocks. The noise of the water frightened Virginia, and she was afraid to wade through the current: Paul therefore took her up in his arms, and went thus loaded over the slippery rocks, which formed the bed of the river, careless of the tumultuous noise of its waters. "Do not be afraid," cried he to Virginia; "I feel very strong with you. If that planter at the Black River had refused you the pardon of his slave, I would have fought with him."--"What!" answered Virginia, "with that great wicked man? To what have I exposed you! Gracious heaven! how difficult it is to do good! and yet it is so easy to do wrong."

When Paul had crossed the river, he wished to continue the journey carrying his sister: and he flattered himself that he could ascend in that way the mountain of the Three Breasts, which was still at the distance of half a league; but his strength soon failed, and he was obliged to set down his burthen, and to rest himself by her side. Virginia then said to him, "My dear brother, the sun is going down; you have still some strength left, but mine has quite failed: do leave me here, and return home alone to ease the fears of our mothers."--"Oh no," said Paul, "I will not leave you if night overtakes us in this wood, I will light a fire, and bring down another palm-tree: you shall eat the cabbage, and I will form a covering of the leaves to shelter you." In the meantime, Virginia being a little rested, she gathered from the trunk of an old tree, which overhung the bank of the river, some long leaves of the plant called hart's tongue, which grew near its root. Of these leaves she made a sort of buskin, with which she covered her feet, that were bleeding from the sharpness of the stony paths; for in her eager desire to do good, she had forgotten to put on her shoes. Feeling her feet cooled by the freshness of the leaves, she broke off a branch of bamboo, and continued her walk, leaning with one hand on the staff, and with the other on Paul.

They walked on in this manner slowly through the woods; but from the height of the trees, and the thickness of their foliage, they soon lost sight of the mountain of the Three Breasts, by which they had hitherto directed their course, and also of the sun, which was now setting. At length they wandered, without perceiving it, from the beaten path in which they had hitherto walked, and found themselves in a labyrinth of trees, underwood, and rocks, whence there appeared to be no outlet. Paul made Virginia sit down, while he ran backwards and forwards, half frantic, in search of a path which might lead them out of this thick wood; but he fatigued himself to no purpose. He then climbed to the top of a lofty tree, whence he hoped at least to perceive the mountain of the Three Breasts: but he could discern nothing around him but the tops of trees, some of which were gilded with the last beams of the setting sun. Already the shadows of the mountains were spreading over the forests in the valleys. The wind lulled, as is usually the case at sunset. The most profound silence reigned in those awful solitudes, which was only interrupted by the cry of the deer, who came to their lairs in that unfrequented spot. Paul, in the hope that some hunter would hear his voice, called out as loud as he was able,--"Come, come to the help of Virginia." But the echoes of the forest alone answered his call, and repeated again and again, "Virginia--Virginia."

Paul at length descended from the tree, overcome with fatigue and vexation. He looked around in order to make some arrangement for passing the night in that desert; but he could find neither fountain, nor palm-tree, nor even a branch of dry wood fit for kindling a fire. He was then impressed, by experience, with the sense of his own weakness, and began to weep. Virginia said to him,--"Do not weep, my dear brother, or I shall be overwhelmed with grief. I am the cause of all your sorrow, and of all that our mothers are suffering at this moment. I find we ought to do nothing, not even good, without consulting our parents. Oh, I have been very imprudent!"--and she began to shed tears. "Let us pray to God, my dear brother," she again said, "and he will hear us." They had scarcely finished their prayer, when they heard the barking of a dog. "It must be the dog of some hunter," said Paul, "who comes here at night, to lie in wait for the deer." Soon after, the dog began barking again with increased violence. "Surely," said Virginia, "it is Fidele, our own dog: yes,--now I know his bark. Are we then so near home?--at the foot of our own mountain?" A moment after, Fidele was at their feet, barking, howling, moaning, and devouring them with his caresses. Before they could recover from their surprise, they saw Domingo running towards them. At the sight of the good old negro, who wept for joy, they began to weep too, but had not the power to utter a syllable. When Domingo had recovered himself a little,--"Oh, my dear children," said he, "how miserable have you made your mothers! How astonished they were when they returned with me from mass, on not finding you at home. Mary, who was at work at a little distance, could not tell us where you were gone. I ran backwards and forwards in the plantation, not knowing where to look for you. At last I took some of your old clothes, and showing them to Fidele, the poor animal, as if he understood me, immediately began to scent your path; and conducted me, wagging his tail all the while, to the Black River. I there saw a planter, who told me you had brought back a Maroon negro woman, his slave, and that he had pardoned her at your request. But what a pardon! he showed her to me with her feet chained to a block of wood, and an iron collar with three hooks fastened round her neck! After that, Fidele, still on the scent, led me up the steep bank of the Black River, where he again stopped, and barked with all his might. This was on the brink of a spring, near which was a fallen palm-tree, and a fire, still smoking. At last he led me to this very spot. We are now at the foot of the mountain of the Three Breasts, and still a good four leagues from home. Come, eat, and recover your strength." Domingo then presented them with a cake, some fruit, and a large gourd, full of beverage composed of wine, water, lemon-juice, sugar, and nutmeg, which their mothers had prepared to invigorate and refresh them. Virginia sighed at the recollection of the poor slave, and at the uneasiness they had given their mothers. She repeated several times--"Oh, how difficult it is to do good!" While she and Paul were taking refreshment, it being already night, Domingo kindled a fire: and having found among the rocks a particular kind of twisted wood, called bois de ronde, which burns when quite green, and throws out a great blaze, he made a torch of it, which he lighted. But when they prepared to continue their journey, a new difficulty occurred; Paul and Virginia could no longer walk, their feet being violently swollen and inflamed. Domingo knew not what to do; whether to leave them and go in search of help, or remain and pass the night with them on that spot. "There was a time," said he, "when I could carry you both together in my arms! But now you are grown big, and I am grown old." When he was in this perplexity, a troop of Maroon negroes appeared at a short distance from them. The chief of the band, approaching Paul and Virginia, said to them,--"Good little white people, do not be afraid. We saw you pass this morning, with a negro woman of the Black River. You went to ask pardon for her of her wicked master; and we, in return for this, will carry you home upon our shoulders." He then made a sign, and four of the strongest negroes immediately formed a sort of litter with the branches of trees and lianas, and having seated Paul and Virginia on it, carried them upon their shoulders. Domingo marched in front with his lighted torch, and they proceeded amidst the rejoicings of the whole troop, who overwhelmed them with their benedictions. Virginia, affected by this scene, said to Paul, with emotion,--"Oh, my dear brother! God never leaves a good action unrewarded."

It was midnight when they arrived at the foot of their mountain, on the ridges of which several fires were lighted. As soon as they began to ascend, they heard voices exclaiming--"Is it you, my children?" They answered immediately, and the negroes also,--"Yes, yes, it is." A moment after they could distinguish their mothers and Mary coming towards them with lighted sticks in their hands. "Unhappy children," cried Madame de la Tour, "where have you been? What agonies you have made us suffer!"--"We have been," said Virginia, "to the Black River, where we went to ask pardon for a poor Maroon slave, to whom I gave our breakfast this morning, because she seemed dying of hunger; and these Maroon negroes have brought us home." Madame de la Tour embraced her daughter, without being able to speak; and Virginia, who felt her face wet with her mother's tears, exclaimed, "Now I am repaid for all the hardships I have suffered." Margaret, in a transport of delight, pressed Paul in her arms, exclaiming, "And you also, my dear child, you have done a good action." When they reached the cottages with their children, they entertained all the negroes with a plentiful repast, after which the latter returned to the woods, praying Heaven to shower down every description of blessing on those good white people.

Every day was to these families a day of happiness and tranquillity. Neither ambition nor envy disturbed their repose. They did not seek to obtain a useless reputation out of doors, which may be procured by artifice and lost by calumny; but were contented to be the sole witnesses and judges of their own actions. In this island, where, as is the case in most colonies, scandal forms the principal topic of conversation, their virtues, and even their names were unknown. The passer-by on the road to Shaddock Grove, indeed, would sometimes ask the inhabitants of the plain, who lived in the cottages up there? and was always told, even by those who did not know them, "They are good people." The modest violet thus, concealed in thorny places sheds all unseen its delightful fragrance around.

Slander, which, under an appearance of justice, naturally inclines the heart to falsehood or to hatred, was entirely banished from their conversation; for it is impossible not to hate men if we believe them to be wicked, or to live with the wicked without concealing that hatred under a false pretence of good feeling. Slander thus puts us ill at ease with others and with ourselves. In this little circle, therefore, the conduct of individuals was not discussed, but the best manner of doing good to all; and although they had but little in their power, their unceasing good-will and kindness of heart made them constantly ready to do what they could for others. Solitude, far from having blunted these benevolent feelings, had rendered their dispositions even more kindly. Although the petty scandals of the day furnished no subject of conversation to them, yet the contemplation of nature filled their minds with enthusiastic delight. They adored the bounty of that Providence, which, by their instrumentality, had spread abundance and beauty amid these barren rocks, and had enabled them to enjoy those pure and simple pleasures, which are ever grateful and ever new.

Paul, at twelve years of age, was stronger and more intelligent than most European youths are at fifteen; and the plantations, which Domingo merely cultivated, were embellished by him. He would go with the old negro into the neighbouring woods, where he would root up the young plants of lemon, orange, and tamarind trees, the round heads of which are so fresh a green, together with date-palm trees, which produce fruit filled with a sweet cream, possessing the fine perfume of the orange flower. These trees, which had already attained to a considerable size, he planted round their little enclosure. He had also sown the seed of many trees which the second year bear flowers or fruit; such as the agathis, encircled with long clusters of white flowers which hang from it like the crystal pendants of a chandelier; the Persian lilac, which lifts high in air its gray flax-coloured branches; the pappaw tree, the branchless trunk of which forms a column studded with green melons, surmounted by a capital of broad leaves similar to those of the fig-tree.

The seeds and kernels of the gum tree, terminalia, mango, alligator pear, the guava, the bread-fruit tree, and the narrow-leaved rose-apple, were also planted by him with profusion: and the greater number of these trees already afforded their young cultivator both shade and fruit. His industrious hands diffused the riches of nature over even the most barren parts of the plantation. Several species of aloes, the Indian fig, adorned with yellow flowers spotted with red, and the thorny torch thistle, grew upon the dark summits of the rocks, and seemed to aim at reaching the long lianas, which, laden with blue or scarlet flowers, hung scattered over the steepest parts of the mountain.

I loved to trace the ingenuity he had exercised in the arrangement of these trees. He had so disposed them that the whole could be seen at a single glance. In the middle of the hollow he had planted shrubs of the lowest growth; behind grew the more lofty sorts; then trees of the ordinary height; and beyond and above all, the venerable and lofty groves which border the circumference. Thus this extensive enclosure appeared, from its centre, like a verdant amphitheatre decorated with fruits and flowers, containing a variety of vegetables, some strips of meadow land, and fields of rice and corn. But, in arranging these vegetable productions to his own taste, he wandered not too far from the designs of Nature. Guided by her suggestions, he had thrown upon the elevated spots such seeds as the winds would scatter about, and near the borders of the springs those which float upon the water. Every plant thus grew in its proper soil, and every spot seemed decorated by Nature's own hand. The streams which fell from the summits of the rocks formed in some parts of the valley sparkling cascades, and in others were spread into broad mirrors, in which were reflected, set in verdure, the flowering trees, the overhanging rocks, and the azure heavens.

Notwithstanding the great irregularity of the ground, these plantations were, for the most part, easy of access. We had, indeed, all given him our advice and assistance, in order to accomplish this end. He had conducted one path entirely round the valley, and various branches from it led from the circumference to the centre. He had drawn some advantage from the most rugged spots, and had blended, in harmonious union, level walks with the inequalities of the soil, and trees which grow wild with the cultivated varieties. With that immense quantity of large pebbles which now block up these paths, and which are scattered over most of the ground of this island, he formed pyramidal heaps here and there, at the base of which he laid mould, and planted rose-bushes, the Barbadoes flower-fence, and other shrubs which love to climb the rocks. In a short time the dark and shapeless heaps of stones he had constructed were covered with verdure, or with the glowing tints of the most beautiful flowers. Hollow recesses on the borders of the streams shaded by the overhanging boughs of aged trees, formed rural grottoes, impervious to the rays of the sun, in which you might enjoy a refreshing coolness during the mid-day heats. One path led to a clump of forest trees, in the centre of which sheltered from the wind, you found a fruit-tree, laden with produce. Here was a corn-field; there, an orchard; from one avenue you had a view of the cottages; from another, of the inaccessible summit of the mountain. Beneath one tufted bower of gum trees, interwoven with lianas, no object whatever could be perceived: while the point of the adjoining rock, jutting out from the mountain, commanded a view of the whole enclosure, and of the distant ocean, where, occasionally, we could discern the distant sail, arriving from Europe, or bound thither. On this rock the two families frequently met in the evening, and enjoyed in silence the freshness of the flowers, the gentle murmurs of the fountain, and the last blended harmonies of light and shade.

Nothing could be more charming than the names which were bestowed upon some of the delightful retreats of this labyrinth. The rock of which I have been speaking, whence they could discern my approach at a considerable distance, was called the Discovery of Friendship. Paul and Virginia had amused themselves by planting a bamboo on that spot; and whenever they saw me coming, they hoisted a little white handkerchief, by way of signal of my approach, as they had seen a flag hoisted on the neighbouring mountain on the sight of a vessel at sea. The idea struck me of engraving an inscription on the stalk of this reed; for I never, in the course of my travels, experienced any thing like the pleasure in seeing a statue or other monument of ancient art, as in reading a well-written inscription. It seems to me as if a human voice issued from the stone, and, making itself heard after the lapse of ages, addressed man in the midst of a desert, to tell him that he is not alone, and that other men, on that very spot, had felt, and thought, and suffered like himself. If the inscription belongs to an ancient nation, which no longer exists, it leads the soul through infinite space, and strengthens the consciousness of its immortality, by demonstrating that a thought has survived the ruins of an empire.

I inscribed then, on the little staff of Paul and Virginia's flag, the following lines of Horace:--

Fratres Helenae, lucida sidera,
Ventorumque regat pater,
Obstrictis, aliis, praeter Iapiga.

"May the brothers of Helen, bright stars like you, and the Father of the winds, guide you; and may you feel only the breath of the zephyr."

There was a gum-tree, under the shade of which Paul was accustomed to sit, to contemplate the sea when agitated by storms. On the bark of this tree, I engraved the following lines from Virgil:--

Fortunatus et ille deos qui novit agrestes!
"Happy are thou, my son, in knowing only the pastoral divinities."

And over the door of Madame de la Tour's cottage where the families so frequently met, I placed this line:--

At secura quies, et nescia fallere vita.
"Here dwell a calm conscience, and a life that knows not deceit."

But Virginia did not approve of my Latin: she said, that what I had placed at the foot of her flagstaff was too long and too learned. "I should have liked better," added she, "to have seen inscribed, EVER AGITATED, YET CONSTANT."--"Such a motto," I answered, "would have been still more applicable to virtue." My reflection made her blush.

The delicacy of sentiment of these happy families was manifested in every thing around them. They gave the tenderest names to objects in appearance the most indifferent. A border of orange, plantain and rose-apple trees, planted round a green sward where Virginia and Paul sometimes danced, received the name of Concord. An old tree, beneath the shade of which Madame de la Tour and Margaret used to recount their misfortunes, was called the Burial-place of Tears. They bestowed the names of Brittany and Normandy on two little plots of ground, where they had sown corn, strawberries, and peas. Domingo and Mary, wishing, in imitation of their mistresses, to recall to mind Angola and Foullepoint, the places of their birth in Africa, gave those names to the little fields where the grass was sown with which they wove their baskets, and where they had planted a calabash-tree. Thus, by cultivating the productions of their respective climates, these exiled families cherished the dear illusions which bind us to our native country, and softened their regrets in a foreign land. Alas! I have seen these trees, these fountains, these heaps of stones, which are now so completely overthrown,--which now, like the desolated plains of Greece, present nothing but masses of ruin and affecting remembrances, all called into life by the many charming appellations thus bestowed upon them!

But perhaps the most delightful spot of this enclosure was that called Virginia's resting-place. At the foot of the rock which bore the name of The Discovery of Friendship, is a small crevice, whence issues a fountain, forming, near its source, a little spot of marshy soil in the middle of a field of rich grass. At the time of Paul's birth I had made Margaret a present of an Indian cocoa which had been given me, and which she planted on the border of this fenny ground, in order that the tree might one day serve to mark the epoch of her son's birth. Madame de la Tour planted another cocoa with the same view, at the birth of Virginia. These nuts produced two cocoa-trees, which formed the only records of the two families; one was called Paul's tree, the other, Virginia's. Their growth was in the same proportion as that of the two young persons, not exactly equal: but they rose, at the end of twelve years, above the roofs of the cottages. Already their tender stalks were interwoven, and clusters of young cocoas hung from them over the basin of the fountain. With the exception of these two trees, this nook of the rock was left as it had been decorated by nature. On its embrowned and moist sides broad plants of maiden-hair glistened with their green and dark stars; and tufts of wave-leaved hart's tongue, suspended like long ribands of purpled green, floated on the wind. Near this grew a chain of the Madagascar periwinkle, the flowers of which resemble the red gilliflower; and the long-podded capsicum, the seed-vessels of which are of the colour of blood, and more resplendent than coral. Near them, the herb balm, with its heart-shaped leaves, and the sweet basil, which has the odour of the clove, exhaled the most delicious perfumes. From the precipitous side of the mountain hung the graceful lianas, like floating draperies, forming magnificent canopies of verdure on the face of the rocks. The sea-birds, allured by the stillness of these retreats, resorted here to pass the night. At the hour of sunset we could perceive the curlew and the stint skimming along the seashore; the frigate-bird poised high in air; and the white bird of the tropic, which abandons, with the star of day, the solitudes of the Indian ocean. Virginia took pleasure in resting herself upon the border of this fountain, decorated with wild and sublime magnificence. She often went thither to wash the linen of the family beneath the shade of the two cocoa-trees, and thither too she sometimes led her goats to graze. While she was making cheeses of their milk, she loved to see them browse on the maiden-hair fern which clothes the steep sides of the rock, and hung suspended by one of its cornices, as on a pedestal. Paul, observing that Virginia was fond of this spot, brought thither, from the neighbouring forest, a great variety of bird's nests. The old birds following their young, soon established themselves in this new colony. Virginia, at stated times, distributed amongst them grains of rice, millet, and maize. As soon as she appeared, the whistling blackbird, the amadavid bird, whose note is so soft, the cardinal, with its flame coloured plumage, forsook their bushes; the parroquet, green as an emerald, descended from the neighbouring fan-palms, the partridge ran along the grass; all advanced promiscuously towards her, like a brood of chickens: and she and Paul found an exhaustless source of amusement in observing their sports, their repasts, and their loves.

Amiable children! thus passed your earlier days in innocence, and in obeying the impulses of kindness. How many times, on this very spot, have your mothers, pressing you in their arms, blessed Heaven for the consolation your unfolding virtues prepared for their declining years, while they at the same time enjoyed the satisfaction of seeing you begin life under the happiest auspices! How many times, beneath the shade of those rocks, have I partaken with them of your rural repasts, which never cost any animal its life! Gourds full of milk, fresh eggs, cakes of rice served up on plantain leaves, with baskets of mangoes, oranges, dates, pomegranates, pineapples, furnished a wholesome repast, the most agreeable to the eye, as well as delicious to the taste, that can possibly be imagined.

Like the repast, the conversation was mild, and free from every thing having a tendency to do harm. Paul often talked of the labours of the day and of the morrow. He was continually planning something for the accommodation of their little society. Here he discovered that the paths were rugged; there, that the seats were uncomfortable: sometimes the young arbours did not afford sufficient shade, and Virginia might be better pleased elsewhere.

During the rainy season the two families met together in the cottage, and employed themselves in weaving mats of grass, and baskets of bamboo. Rakes, spades, and hatchets, were ranged along the walls in the most perfect order; and near these instruments of agriculture were heaped its products,--bags of rice, sheaves of corn, and baskets of plantains. Some degree of luxury usually accompanies abundance; and Virginia was taught by her mother and Margaret to prepare sherbert and cordials from the juice of the sugar-cane, the lemon and the citron.

When night came, they all supped together by the light of a lamp; after which Madame de la Tour or Margaret related some story of travellers benighted in those woods of Europe that are still infested by banditti; or told a dismal tale of some shipwrecked vessel, thrown by the tempest upon the rocks of a desert island. To these recitals the children listened with eager attention, and earnestly hoped that Heaven would one day grant them the joy of performing the rites of hospitality towards such unfortunate persons. When the time for repose arrived, the two families separated and retired for the night, eager to meet again the following morning. Sometimes they were lulled to repose by the beating of the rains, which fell in torrents upon the roofs of their cottages, and sometimes by the hollow winds, which brought to their ear the distant roar of the waves breaking upon the shore. They blessed God for their own safety, the feeling of which was brought home more forcibly to their minds by the sound of remote danger.

Madame de la Tour occasionally read aloud some affecting history of the Old or New Testament. Her auditors reasoned but little upon these sacred volumes, for their theology centred in a feeling of devotion towards the Supreme Being, like that of nature: and their morality was an active principle, like that of the Gospel. These families had no particular days devoted to pleasure, and others to sadness. Every day was to them a holyday, and all that surrounded them one holy temple, in which they ever adored the Infinite Intelligence, the Almighty God, the Friend of human kind. A feeling of confidence in his supreme power filled their minds with consolation for the past, with fortitude under present trials, and with hope in the future. Compelled by misfortune to return almost to a state of nature, these excellent women had thus developed in their own and their children's bosoms the feelings most natural to the human mind, and its best support under affliction.

But, as clouds sometimes arise, and cast a gloom over the best regulated tempers, so whenever any member of this little society appeared to be labouring under dejection, the rest assembled around, and endeavoured to banish her painful thoughts by amusing the mind rather than by grave arguments against them. Each performed this kind office in their own appropriate manner: Margaret, by her gaiety; Madame de la Tour, by the gentle consolations of religion; Virginia, by her tender caresses; Paul, by his frank and engaging cordiality. Even Mary and Domingo hastened to offer their succour, and to weep with those that wept. Thus do weak plants interweave themselves with each other, in order to withstand the fury of the tempest.

During the fine season, they went every Sunday to the church of the Shaddock Grove, the steeple of which you see yonder upon the plain. Many wealthy members of the congregation, who came to church in palanquins, sought the acquaintance of these united families, and invited them to parties of pleasure. But they always repelled these overtures with respectful politeness, as they were persuaded that the rich and powerful seek the society of persons in an inferior station only for the sake of surrounding themselves with flatterers, and that every flatterer must applaud alike all the actions of his patron, whether good or bad. On the other hand, they avoided, with equal care, too intimate an acquaintance with the lower class, who are ordinarily jealous, calumniating, and gross. They thus acquired, with some, the character of being timid, and with others, of pride: but their reserve was accompanied with so much obliging politeness, above all towards the unfortunate and the unhappy, that they insensibly acquired the respect of the rich and the confidence of the poor.

After service, some kind office was often required at their hands by their poor neighbours. Sometimes a person troubled in mind sought their advice; sometimes a child begged them to its sick mother, in one of the adjoining hamlets. They always took with them a few remedies for the ordinary diseases of the country, which they administered in that soothing manner which stamps a value upon the smallest favours. Above all, they met with singular success in administrating to the disorders of the mind, so intolerable in solitude, and under the infirmities of a weakened frame. Madame de la Tour spoke with such sublime confidence of the Divinity, that the sick, while listening to her, almost believed him present. Virginia often returned home with her eyes full of tears, and her heart overflowing with delight, at having had an opportunity of doing good; for to her generally was confided the task of preparing and administering the medicines,--a task which she fulfilled with angelic sweetness. After these visits of charity, they sometimes extended their walk by the Sloping Mountain, till they reached my dwelling, where I used to prepare dinner for them on the banks of the little rivulet which glides near my cottage. I procured for these occasions a few bottles of old wine, in order to heighten the relish of our Oriental repast by the more genial productions of Europe. At other times we met on the sea-shore, at the mouth of some little river, or rather mere brook. We brought from home the provisions furnished us by our gardens, to which we added those supplied us by the sea in abundant variety. We caught on these shores the mullet, the roach, and the sea-urchin, lobsters, shrimps, crabs, oysters, and all other kinds of shell-fish. In this way, we often enjoyed the most tranquil pleasures in situations the most terrific. Sometimes, seated upon a rock, under the shade of the velvet sunflower-tree, we saw the enormous waves of the Indian Ocean break beneath our feet with a tremendous noise. Paul, who could swim like a fish, would advance on the reefs to meet the coming billows; then, at their near approach, would run back to the beach, closely pursued by the foaming breakers, which threw themselves, with a roaring noise, far on the sands. But Virginia, at this sight, uttered piercing cries, and said that such sports frightened her too much.

Other amusements were not wanting on these festive occasions. Our repasts were generally followed by the songs and dances of the two young people. Virginia sang the happiness of pastoral life, and the misery of those who were impelled by avarice to cross the raging ocean, rather than cultivate the earth, and enjoy its bounties in peace. Sometimes she performed a pantomime with Paul, after the manner of the negroes. The first language of man is pantomime: it is known to all nations, and is so natural and expressive, that the children of the European inhabitants catch it with facility from the negroes. Virginia, recalling, from among the histories which her mother had read to her, those which had affected her most, represented the principal events in them with beautiful simplicity. Sometimes at the sound of Domingo's tantam she appeared upon the green sward, bearing a pitcher upon her head, and advanced with a timid step towards the source of a neighbouring fountain, to draw water. Domingo and Mary, personating the shepherds of Midian forbade her to approach, and repulsed her sternly. Upon this Paul flew to her succour, beat away the shepherds, filled Virginia's pitcher, and placing it upon her heard, bound her brows at the same time with a wreath of the red flowers of the Madagascar periwinkle, which served to heighten the delicacy of her complexion. Then joining in their sports, I took upon myself the part of Raguel, and bestowed upon Paul, my daughter Zephora in marriage.

Another time Virginia would represent the unhappy Ruth, returning poor and widowed with her mother-in-law, who, after so prolonged an absence, found herself as unknown as in a foreign land. Domingo and Mary personated the reapers. The supposed daughter of Naomi followed their steps, gleaning here and there a few ears of corn. When interrogated by Paul,--a part which he performed with the gravity of a patriarch,--she answered his questions with a faltering voice. He then, touched with compassion, granted an asylum to innocence, and hospitality to misfortune. He filled her lap with plenty; and, leading her towards us as before the elders of the city, declared his purpose to take her in marriage. At this scene, Madame de la Tour, recalling the desolate situation in which she had been left by her relations, her widowhood, and the kind reception she had met with from Margaret, succeeded now by the soothing hope of a happy union between their children, could not forbear weeping; and these mixed recollections of good and evil caused us all to unite with her in shedding tears of sorrow and of joy.

These dramas were performed with such an air of reality that you might have fancied yourself transported to the plains of Syria or of Palestine. We were not unfurnished with decorations, lights, or an orchestra, suitable to the representation. The scene was generally placed in an open space of the forest, the diverging paths from which formed around us numerous arcades of foliage, under which we were sheltered from the heat all the middle of the day; but when the sun descended towards the horizon, its rays, broken by the trunks of the trees, darted amongst the shadows of the forest in long lines of light, producing the most magnificent effect. Sometimes its broad disk appeared at the end of an avenue, lighting it up with insufferable brightness. The foliage of the trees, illuminated from beneath by its saffron beams, glowed with the lustre of the topaz and the emerald. Their brown and mossy trunks appeared transformed into columns of antique bronze; and the birds, which had retired in silence to their leafy shades to pass the night, surprised to see the radiance of a second morning, hailed the star of day all together with innumerable carols.

Night often overtook us during these rural entertainments; but the purity of the air and the warmth of the climate, admitted of our sleeping in the woods, without incurring any danger by exposure to the weather, and no less secure from the molestations of robbers. On our return the following day to our respective habitations, we found them in exactly the same state in which they had been left. In this island, then unsophisticated by the pursuits of commerce, such were the honesty and primitive manners of the population, that the doors of many houses were without a key, and even a lock itself was an object of curiosity to not a few of the native inhabitants.

There were, however, some days in the year celebrated by Paul and Virginia in a more peculiar manner; these were the birth-days of their mothers. Virginia never failed the day before to prepare some wheaten cakes, which she distributed among a few poor white families, born in the island, who had never eaten European bread. These unfortunate people, uncared for by the blacks, were reduced to live on tapioca in the woods; and as they had neither the insensibility which is the result of slavery, nor the fortitude which springs from a liberal education, to enable them to support their poverty, their situation was deplorable. These cakes were all that Virginia had it in her power to give away, but she conferred the gift in so delicate a manner as to add tenfold to its value. In the first place, Paul was commissioned to take the cakes himself to these families, and get their promise to come and spend the next day at Madame de la Tour's. Accordingly, mothers of families, with two or three thin, yellow, miserable looking daughters, so timid that they dared not look up, made their appearance. Virginia soon put them at their ease; she waited upon them with refreshments, the excellence of which she endeavoured to heighten by relating some particular circumstance which in her own estimation, vastly improved them. One beverage had been prepared by Margaret; another, by her mother: her brother himself had climbed some lofty tree for the very fruit she was presenting. She would then get Paul to dance with them, nor would she leave them till she saw that they were happy. She wished them to partake of the joy of her own family. "It is only," she said, "by promoting the happiness of others, that we can secure our own." When they left, she generally presented them with some little article they seemed to fancy, enforcing their acceptance of it by some delicate pretext, that she might not appear to know they were in want. If she remarked that their clothes were much tattered, she obtained her mother's permission to give them some of her own, and then sent Paul to leave them, secretly at their cottage doors. She thus followed the divine precept,--concealing the benefactor, and revealing only the benefit.

You Europeans, whose minds are imbued from infancy with prejudices at variance with happiness, cannot imagine all the instruction and pleasure to be derived from nature. Your souls, confined to a small sphere of intelligence, soon reach the limit of its artificial enjoyments: but nature and the heart are inexhaustible. Paul and Virginia had neither clock, nor almanack, nor books of chronology, history or philosophy. The periods of their lives were regulated by those of the operations of nature, and their familiar conversation had a reference to the changes of the seasons. They knew the time of day by the shadows of the trees; the seasons, by the times when those trees bore flowers or fruit; and the years, by the number of their harvests. These soothing images diffused an inexpressible charm over their conversation. "It is time to dine," said Virginia, "the shadows of the plantain-trees are at their roots:" or, "Night approaches, the tamarinds are closing their leaves." "When will you come and see us?" inquired some of her companions in the neighbourhood. "At the time of the sugar-canes," answered Virginia. "Your visit will be then still more delightful," resumed her young acquaintances. When she was asked what was her own age and that of Paul,--"My brother," said she, "is as old as the great cocoa-tree of the fountain; and I am as old as the little one: the mangoes have bore fruit twelve times and the orange-trees have flowered four-and-twenty times, since I came into the world." Their lives seemed linked to that of the trees, like those of Fauns or Dryads. They knew no other historical epochs than those of the lives of their mothers, no other chronology than that of doing good, and resigning themselves to the will of Heaven.

What need, indeed, had these young people of riches or learning such as ours? Even their necessities and their ignorance increased their happiness. No day passed in which they were not of some service to one another, or in which they did not mutually impart some instruction. Yes, instruction; for if errors mingled with it, they were, at least, not of a dangerous character. A pure-minded being has none of that description to fear. Thus grew these children of nature. No care had troubled their peace, no intemperance had corrupted their blood, no misplaced passion had depraved their hearts. Love, innocence, and piety, possessed their souls; and those intellectual graces were unfolding daily in their features, their attitudes, and their movements. Still in the morning of life, they had all its blooming freshness: and surely such in the garden of Eden appeared our first parents, when coming from the hands of God, they first saw, and approached each other, and conversed together, like brother and sister. Virginia was gentle, modest, and confiding as Eve; and Paul, like Adam, united the stature of manhood with the simplicity of a child.

Sometimes, if alone with Virginia, he has a thousand times told me, he used to say to her, on his return from labour,--"When I am wearied, the sight of you refreshes me. If from the summit of the mountain I perceive you below in the valley, you appear to me in the midst of our orchard like a blooming rose-bud. If you go towards our mother's house, the partridge, when it runs to meet its young, has a shape less beautiful, and a step less light. When I lose sight of you through the trees, I have no need to see you in order to find you again. Something of you, I know not how, remains for me in the air through which you have passed, on the grass where you have been seated. When I come near you, you delight all my senses. The azure of the sky is less charming than the blue of your eyes, and the song of the amadavid bird less soft than the sound of your voice. If I only touch you with the tip of my finger, my whole frame trembles with pleasure. Do you remember the day when

we crossed over the great stones of the river of the Three Breasts? I was very tired
before we reached the bank: but, as soon as I had taken you in my arms, I seemed
to have wings like a bird. Tell me by what charm you have thus enchanted me! Is it
by your wisdom?--Our mothers have more than either of us. Is it by your caresses?-
-They embrace me much oftener than you. I think it must be by your goodness. I
shall never forget how you walked bare-footed to the Black River, to ask pardon for
the poor run-away slave. Here, my beloved, take this flowering branch of a lemon-
tree, which I have gathered in the forest: you will let it remain at night near your
bed. Eat this honey-comb too, which I have taken for you from the top of a rock.
But first lean on my bosom, and I shall be refreshed."

Virginia would answer him,--"Oh, my dear brother, the rays of the sun in the
morning on the tops of the rocks give me less joy than the sight of you. I love my
mother,--I love yours; but when they call you their son, I love them a thousand
times more. When they caress you, I feel it more sensibly than when I am caressed
myself. You ask me what makes you love me. Why, all creatures that are brought
up together love one another. Look at our birds; reared up in the same nests, they
love each other as we do; they are always together like us. Hark! how they call and
answer from one tree to another. So when the echoes bring to my ears the air which
you play on your flute on the top of the mountain, I repeat the words at the bottom
of the valley. You are dear to me more especially since the day when you wanted to
fight the master of the slave for me. Since that time how often have I said to myself,
'Ah, my brother has a good heart; but for him, I should have died of terror.' I pray to
God every day for my mother and for yours; for you, and for our poor servants; but
when I pronounce your name, my devotion seems to increase;--I ask so earnestly of
God that no harm may befall you! Why do you go so far, and climb so high, to seek
fruits and flowers for me? Have we not enough in our garden already? How much
you are fatigued,--you look so warm!"--and with her little white handkerchief she
would wipe the damps from his face, and then imprint a tender kiss on his fore-
head.

For some time past, however, Virginia had felt her heart agitated by new sensations. Her beautiful blue eyes lost their lustre, her cheek its freshness, and her
frame was overpowered with a universal langour. Serenity no longer sat upon her
brow, nor smiles played upon her lips. She would become all at once gay without

cause for joy, and melancholy without any subject for grief. She fled her innocent amusements, her gentle toils, and even the society of her beloved family; wandering about the most unfrequented parts of the plantations, and seeking every where the rest which she could no where find. Sometimes, at the sight of Paul, she advanced sportively to meet him; but, when about to accost him, was overcome by a sudden confusion; her pale cheeks were covered with blushes, and her eyes no longer dared to meet those of her brother. Paul said to her,--"The rocks are covered with verdure, our birds begin to sing when you approach, everything around you is gay, and you only are unhappy." He then endeavoured to soothe her by his embraces, but she turned away her head, and fled, trembling towards her mother. The caresses of her brother excited too much emotion in her agitated heart, and she sought, in the arms of her mother, refuge from herself. Paul, unused to the secret windings of the female heart, vexed himself in vain in endeavouring to comprehend the meaning of these new and strange caprices. Misfortunes seldom come alone, and a serious calamity now impended over these families.

One of those summers, which sometimes desolate the countries situated between the tropics, now began to spread its ravages over this island. It was near the end of December, when the sun, in Capricorn, darts over the Mauritius, during the space of three weeks, its vertical fires. The southeast wind, which prevails throughout almost the whole year, no longer blew. Vast columns of dust arose from the highways, and hung suspended in the air; the ground was every where broken into clefts; the grass was burnt up; hot exhalations issued from the sides of the mountains, and their rivulets, for the most part, became dry. No refreshing cloud ever arose from the sea: fiery vapours, only, during the day, ascended from the plains, and appeared, at sunset, like the reflection of a vast conflagration. Night brought no coolness to the heated atmosphere; and the red moon rising in the misty horizon, appeared of supernatural magnitude. The drooping cattle, on the sides of the hills, stretching out their necks towards heaven, and panting for breath, made the valleys re-echo with their melancholy lowings: even the Caffre by whom they were led threw himself upon the earth, in search of some cooling moisture: but his hopes were vain; the scorching sun had penetrated the whole soil, and the stifling atmosphere everywhere resounded with the buzzing noise of insects, seeking to allay their thirst with the blood of men and of animals.

During this sultry season, Virginia's restlessness and disquietude were much increased. One night, in particular, being unable to sleep, she arose from her bed, sat down, and returned to rest again; but could find in no attitude either slumber or repose. At length she bent her way, by the light of the moon, towards her fountain, and gazed at its spring, which, notwithstanding the drought, still trickled, in silver threads down the brown sides of the rock. She flung herself into the basin: its coolness reanimated her spirits, and a thousand soothing remembrances came to her mind. She recollected that in her infancy her mother and Margaret had amused themselves by bathing her with Paul in this very spot; that he afterwards, reserving this bath for her sole use, had hollowed out its bed, covered the bottom with sand, and sown aromatic herbs around its borders. She saw in the water, upon her naked arms and bosom, the reflection of the two cocoa trees which were planted at her own and her brother's birth, and which interwove above her head their green branches and young fruit. She thought of Paul's friendship, sweeter than the odour of the blossoms, purer than the waters of the fountain, stronger than the intertwining palm-tree, and she sighed. Reflecting on the hour of the night, and the profound solitude, her imagination became disturbed. Suddenly she flew, affrighted, from those dangerous shades, and those waters which seemed to her hotter than the tropical sunbeam, and ran to her mother for refuge. More than once, wishing to reveal her sufferings, she pressed her mother's hand within her own; more than once she was ready to pronounce the name of Paul: but her oppressed heart left her lips no power of utterance, and, leaning her head on her mother's bosom, she bathed it with her tears.

Madame de la Tour, though she easily discerned the source of her daughter's uneasiness, did not think proper to speak to her on the subject. "My dear child," said she, "offer up your supplications to God, who disposes at his will of health and of life. He subjects you to trial now, in order to recompense you hereafter. Remember that we are only placed upon earth for the exercise of virtue."

The excessive heat in the meantime raised vast masses of vapour from the ocean, which hung over the island like an immense parasol, and gathered round the summits of the mountains. Long flakes of fire issued from time to time from these mist-embosomed peaks. The most awful thunder soon after re-echoed through the woods, the plains, and the valleys: the rains fell from the skies in cataracts; foaming torrents rushed down the sides of this mountain; the bottom of the valley became a sea, and the elevated platform on which the cottages were built, a little island. The accumulated waters, having no other outlet, rushed with violence through the narrow gorge which leads into the valley, tossing and roaring, and bearing along with them a mingled wreck of soil, trees, and rocks.

The trembling families meantime addressed their prayers to God all together in the cottage of Madame de la Tour, the roof of which cracked fearfully from the force of the winds. So incessant and vivid were the lightnings, that although the doors and window-shutters were securely fastened, every object without could be distinctly seen through the joints in the wood-work! Paul, followed by Domingo, went with intrepidity from one cottage to another, notwithstanding the fury of the tempest; here supporting a partition with a buttress, there driving in a stake; and only returning to the family to calm their fears, by the expression of a hope that the storm was passing away. Accordingly, in the evening the rains ceased, the trade-winds of the southeast pursued their ordinary course, the tempestuous clouds were driven away to the northward, and the setting sun appeared in the horizon.

Virginia's first wish was to visit the spot called her Resting-place. Paul approached her with a timid air, and offered her the assistance of his arm; she accepted it with a smile, and they left the cottage together. The air was clear and fresh: white vapours arose from the ridges of the mountain, which was furrowed here and there by the courses of torrents, marked in foam, and now beginning to dry up on all sides. As for the garden, it was completely torn to pieces by deep water-courses, the roots of most of the fruit trees were laid bare, and vast heaps of sand covered the borders of the meadows, and had choked up Virginia's bath. The two cocoa trees, however, were still erect, and still retained their freshness; but they were no longer surrounded by turf, or arbours, or birds, except a few amadavid birds, which, upon the points of the neighbouring rocks, were lamenting, in plaintive notes, the loss of their young.

At the sight of this general desolation, Virginia exclaimed to Paul,--"You brought birds hither, and the hurricane has killed them. You planted this garden, and it is now destroyed. Every thing then upon earth perishes, and it is only Heaven that is not subject to change."--"Why," answered Paul, "cannot I give you something that belongs to Heaven? but I have nothing of my own even upon the earth." Vir-

ginia with a blush replied, "You have the picture of Saint Paul." As soon as she had
uttered the words, he flew in quest of it to his mother's cottage. This picture was a
miniature of Paul the Hermit, which Margaret, who viewed it with feelings of great
devotion, had worn at her neck while a girl, and which, after she became a mother,
she had placed round her child's. It had even happened, that being, while pregnant,
abandoned by all the world, and constantly occupied in contemplating the image
of this benevolent recluse, her offspring had contracted some resemblance to this
revered object. She therefore bestowed upon him the name of Paul, giving him for
his patron a saint who had passed his life far from mankind by whom he had been
first deceived and then forsaken. Virginia, on receiving this little present from the
hands of Paul, said to him, with emotion, "My dear brother, I will never part with
this while I live; nor will I ever forget that you have given me the only thing you
have in the world." At this tone of friendship,--this unhoped for return of familiarity and tenderness, Paul attempted to embrace her; but, light as a bird, she escaped
him, and fled away, leaving him astonished, and unable to account for conduct so
extraordinary.

Meanwhile Margaret said to Madame de la Tour, "Why do we not unite our
children by marriage? They have a strong attachment for each other, and though
my son hardly understands the real nature of his feelings, yet great care and watch-
fulness will be necessary. Under such circumstances, it will be as well not to leave
them too much together." Madame de la Tour replied, "They are too young and too
poor. What grief would it occasion us to see Virginia bring into the world unfortunate children, whom she would not perhaps have sufficient strength to rear! Your
negro, Domingo, is almost too old to labor; Mary is infirm. As for myself, my dear
friend, at the end of fifteen years, I find my strength greatly decreased; the feeble-
ness of age advances rapidly in hot climates, and, above all, under the pressure of
misfortune. Paul is our only hope: let us wait till he comes to maturity, and his increased strength enables him to support us by his labour: at present you well know
that we have only sufficient to supply the wants of the day: but were we to send
Paul for a short time to the Indies, he might acquire, by commerce, the means of
purchasing some slaves; and at his return we could unite him to Virginia; for I am
persuaded no one on earth would render her so happy as your son. We will consult
our neighbour on this subject."

They accordingly asked my advice, which was in accordance with Madame de la Tour's opinion. "The Indian seas," I observed to them, "are calm, and, in choosing a favourable time of the year, the voyage out is seldom longer than six weeks; and the same time may be allowed for the return home. We will furnish Paul with a little venture from my neighbourhood, where he is much beloved. If we were only to supply him with some raw cotton, of which we make no use for want of mills to work it, some ebony, which is here so common that it serves us for firing, and some rosin, which is found in our woods, he would be able to sell those articles, though useless here, to good advantage in the Indies."

I took upon myself to obtain permission from Monsieur de la Bourdonnais to undertake this voyage; and I determined previously to mention the affair to Paul. But what was my surprise, when this young man said to me, with a degree of good sense above his age, "And why do you wish me to leave my family for this precarious pursuit of fortune? Is there any commerce in the world more advantageous than the culture of the ground, which yields sometimes fifty or a hundred-fold? If we wish to engage in commerce, can we not do so by carrying our superfluities to the town without my wandering to the Indies? Our mothers tell me, that Domingo is old and feeble; but I am young, and gather strength every day. If any accident should happen during my absence, above all to Virginia, who already suffers--Oh, no, no!--I cannot resolve to leave them."

So decided an answer threw me into great perplexity, for Madame de la Tour had not concealed from me the cause of Virginia's illness and want of spirits, and her desire of separating these young people till they were a few years older. I took care, however, not to drop any thing which could lead Paul to suspect the existence of these motives.

About this period a ship from France brought Madame de la Tour a letter from her aunt. The fear of death, without which hearts as insensible as hers would never feel, had alarmed her into compassion. When she wrote she was recovering from a dangerous illness, which had, however, left her incurably languid and weak. She desired her niece to return to France: or, if her health forbade her to undertake so long a voyage, she begged her to send Virginia, on whom she promised to bestow a good education, to procure for her a splendid marriage, and to leave her heiress of her whole fortune. She concluded by enjoining strict obedience to her will, in gratitude, she said, for her great kindness.

At the perusal of this letter general consternation spread itself through the whole assembled party. Domingo and Mary began to weep. Paul, motionless with surprise, appeared almost ready to burst with indignation; while Virginia, fixing her eyes anxiously upon her mother, had not power to utter a single word. "And can you now leave us?" cried Margaret to Madame de la Tour. "No, my dear friend, no, my beloved children," replied Madame de la Tour; "I will never leave you. I have lived with you, and with you I will die. I have known no happiness but in your affection. If my health be deranged, my past misfortunes are the cause. My heart has been deeply wounded by the cruelty of my relations, and by the loss of my beloved husband. But I have since found more consolation and more real happiness with you in these humble huts, than all the wealth of my family could now lead me to expect in my country."

At this soothing language every eye overflowed with tears of delight. Paul, pressing Madame de la Tour in his arms, exclaimed,--"Neither will I leave you! I will not go to the Indies. We will all labour for you, dear mamma; and you shall never feel any want with us." But of the whole society, the person who displayed the least transport, and who probably felt the most, was Virginia; and during the remainder of the day, the gentle gaiety which flowed from her heart, and proved that her peace of mind was restored, completed the general satisfaction.

At sun-rise the next day, just as they had concluded offering up, as usual, their morning prayer before breakfast, Domingo came to inform them that a gentleman on horseback, followed by two slaves, was coming towards the plantation. It was Monsieur de la Bourdonnais. He entered the cottage, where he found the family at breakfast. Virginia had prepared, according to the custom of the country, coffee, and rice boiled in water. To these she had added hot yams, and fresh plantains. The leaves of the plantain-tree, supplied the want of table-linen; and calabash shells, split in two, served for cups. The governor exhibited, at first, some astonishment at the homeliness of the dwelling; then, addressing himself to Madame de la Tour, he observed, that although public affairs drew his attention too much from the concerns of individuals, she had many claims on his good offices. "You have an aunt at Paris, madam," he added, "a woman of quality, and immensely rich, who expects that you will hasten to see her, and who means to bestow upon you her whole fortune." Madame de la Tour replied, that the state of her health would not permit her to undertake so long a voyage. "At least," resumed Monsieur de la Bourdonnais, "you cannot without injustice, deprive this amiable young lady, your daughter, of so noble an inheritance. I will not conceal from you, that your aunt has made use of her influence to secure your daughter being sent to her; and that I have received official letters, in which I am ordered to exert my authority, if necessary, to that effect. But as I only wish to employ my power for the purpose of rendering the inhabitants of this country happy, I expect from your good sense the voluntary sacrifice of a few years, upon which your daughter's establishment in the world, and the welfare of your whole life depends. Wherefore do we come to these islands? Is it not to acquire a fortune? And will it not be more agreeable to return and find it in your own country?"

He then took a large bag of piastres from one of his slaves, and placed it upon the table. "This sum," he continued, "is allotted by your aunt to defray the outlay necessary for the equipment of the young lady for her voyage." Gently reproaching Madame de la Tour for not having had recourse to him in her difficulties, he extolled at the same time her noble fortitude. Upon this Paul said to the governor,--"My mother did apply to you, sir, and you received her ill."--"Have you another child, madam?" said Monsieur de la Bourdonnais to Madame de la Tour. "No, Sir," she replied; "this is the son of my friend; but he and Virginia are equally dear to us, and we mutually consider them both as our own children." "Young man," said the governor to Paul, "when you have acquired a little more experience of the world, you will know that it is the misfortune of people in place to be deceived, and bestow, in consequence, upon intriguing vice, that which they would wish to give to modest merit."

Monsieur de la Bourdonnais, at the request of Madame de la Tour, placed himself next to her at table, and breakfasted after the manner of the Creoles, upon coffee, mixed with rice boiled in water. He was delighted with the order and cleanliness which prevailed in the little cottage, the harmony of the two interesting families, and the zeal of their old servants. "Here," he exclaimed, "I discern only wooden furniture; but I find serene countenances and hearts of gold." Paul, enchanted with the affability of the governor, said to him,--"I wish to be your friend: for you are a good man." Monsieur de la Bourdonnais received with pleasure this insular compliment, and, taking Paul by the hand, assured him he might rely upon his friendship.

After breakfast, he took Madame de la Tour aside and informed her that an opportunity would soon offer itself of sending her daughter to France, in a ship which was going to sail in a short time; that he would put her under the charge of a lady, one of the passengers, who was a relation of his own; and that she must not think of renouncing an immense fortune, on account of the pain of being separated from her daughter for a brief interval. "Your aunt," he added, "cannot live more than two years; of this I am assured by her friends. Think of it seriously. Fortune does not visit us every day. Consult your friends. I am sure that every person of good sense will be of my opinion." She answered, "that, as she desired no other happiness henceforth in the world than in promoting that of her daughter, she hoped to be allowed to leave her departure for France to her own inclination."

Madame de la Tour was not sorry to find an opportunity of separating Paul and Virginia for a short time, and provide by this means, for their mutual felicity at a future period. She took her daughter aside, and said to her,--"My dear child, our servants are now old. Paul is still very young, Margaret is advanced in years, and I am already infirm. If I should die what would become of you, without fortune, in the midst of these deserts? You would then be left alone, without any person who could afford you much assistance, and would be obliged to labour without ceasing, as a hired servant, in order to support your wretched existence. This idea overcomes me with sorrow." Virginia answered,--"God has appointed us to labour, and to bless him every day. Up to this time he has never forsaken us, and he never will forsake us in time to come. His providence watches most especially over the unfortunate. You have told me this very often, my dear mother! I cannot resolve to leave you." Madame de la Tour replied, with much emotion,--"I have no other aim than to render you happy, and to marry you one day to Paul, who is not really your brother. Remember then that his fortune depends upon you."

A young girl who is in love believes that every one else is ignorant of her passion; she throws over her eyes the veil with which she covers the feelings of her heart; but when it is once lifted by a friendly hand, the hidden sorrows of her attachment escape as through a newly-opened barrier, and the sweet outpourings of unrestrained confidence succeed to her former mystery and reserve. Virginia, deeply affected by this new proof of her mother's tenderness, related to her the cruel struggles she had undergone, of which heaven alone had been witness; she saw, she said, the hand of Providence in the assistance of an affectionate mother, who approved of her attachment; and would guide her by her counsels; and as she was now strengthened by such support, every consideration led her to remain with her mother, without anxiety for the present, and without apprehension for the future.

Madame de la Tour, perceiving that this confidential conversation had produced an effect altogether different from that which she expected, said,--"My dear child, I do not wish to constrain you; think over it at leisure, but conceal your affection from Paul. It is better not to let a man know that the heart of his mistress is gained."

Virginia and her mother were sitting together by themselves the same evening, when a tall man, dressed in a blue cassock, entered their cottage. He was a missionary priest and the confessor of Madame de la Tour and her daughter, who had now been sent to them by the governor. "My children," he exclaimed as he entered, "God be praised! you are now rich. You can now attend to the kind suggestions of your benevolent hearts, and do good to the poor. I know what Monsieur de la Bourdonnais has said to you, and what you have said in reply. Your health, dear madam, obliges you to remain here; but you, young lady, are without excuse. We must obey our aged relations, even when they are unjust. A sacrifice is required of you; but it is the will of God. Our Lord devoted himself for you; and you in imitation of his example, must give up something for the welfare of your family. Your voyage to France will end happily. You will surely consent to go, my dear young lady."

Virginia, with downcast eyes, answered, trembling, "If it is the command of God, I will not presume to oppose it. Let the will of God be done!" As she uttered these words, she wept.

The priest went away, in order to inform the governor of the success of his mission. In the meantime Madame de la Tour sent Domingo to request me to come to her, that she might consult me respecting Virginia's departure. I was not at all of opinion that she ought to go. I consider it as a fixed principle of happiness, that we ought to prefer the advantages of nature to those of fortune, and never go in search of that at a distance, which we may find at home,--in our own bosoms. But what could be expected from my advice, in opposition to the illusions of a splendid fortune?--or from my simple reasoning, when in competition with the prejudices of the world, and an authority held sacred by Madame de la Tour? This lady indeed only consulted me out of politeness; she had ceased to deliberate since she had heard the decision of her confessor. Margaret herself, who, notwithstanding the advantages she expected for her son from the possession of Virginia's fortune, had hitherto opposed her departure, made no further objections. As for Paul, in ignorance of what had been determined, but alarmed at the secret conversations which Virginia had been holding with her mother, he abandoned himself to melancholy. "They are plotting something against me," cried he, "for they conceal every thing from me."

A report having in the meantime been spread in the island that fortune had visited these rocks, merchants of every description were seen climbing their steep ascent. Now, for the first time, were seen displayed in these humble huts the richest stuffs of India; the fine dimity of Gondelore; the handkerchiefs of Pellicate and Masulipatan; the plain, striped, and embroidered muslins of Dacca, so beautifully transparent: the delicately white cottons of Surat, and linens of all colours. They also brought with them the gorgeous silks of China, satin damasks, some white, and others grass-green and bright red; pink taffetas, with the profusion of satins and gauze of Tonquin, both plain and decorated with flowers; soft pekins, downy as cloth; and white and yellow nankeens, and the calicoes of Madagascar.

Madame de la Tour wished her daughter to purchase whatever she liked; she only examined the goods, and inquired the price, to take care that the dealers did not cheat her. Virginia made choice of everything she thought would be useful or agreeable to her mother, or to Margaret and her son. "This," said she, "will be wanted for furnishing the cottage, and that will be very useful to Mary and Domingo." In short, the bag of piastres was almost emptied before she even began to consider her own wants; and she was obliged to receive back for her own use a share of the presents which she had distributed among the family circle.

Paul, overcome with sorrow at the sight of these gifts of fortune, which he felt were a presage of Virginia's departure, came a few days after to my dwelling. With an air of deep despondency he said to me--"My sister is going away; she is already making preparations for her voyage. I conjure you to come and exert your influence over her mother and mine, in order to detain her here." I could not refuse the young man's solicitations, although well convinced that my representations would be unavailing.

Virginia had ever appeared to me charming when clad in the coarse cloth of Bengal, with a red handkerchief tied round her head: you may therefore imagine how much her beauty was increased, when she was attired in the graceful and elegant costume worn by the ladies of this country! She had on a white muslin dress, lined with pink taffeta. Her somewhat tall and slender figure was shown to advantage in her new attire, and the simple arrangement of her hair accorded admirably with the form of her head. Her fine blue eyes were filled with an expression of melancholy; and the struggles of passion, with which her heart was agitated, imparted a flush to her cheek, and to her voice a tone of deep emotion. The contrast between her pensive look and her gay habiliments rendered her more interesting than ever, nor was it possible to see or hear her unmoved. Paul became more and more melancholy; and at length Margaret, distressed at the situation of her son, took him aside and said to him,--"Why, my dear child, will you cherish vain hopes, which will only render your disappointment more bitter? It is time for me to make known to you the secret of your life and of mine. Mademoiselle de la Tour belongs, by her mother's side, to a rich and noble family, while you are but the son of a poor peasant girl; and what is worse you are illegitimate."

Paul, who had never heard this last expression before, inquired with eagerness its meaning. His mother replied, "I was not married to your father. When I was a girl, seduced by love, I was guilty of a weakness of which you are the offspring. The consequence of my fault is, that you are deprived of the protection of a father's family, and by my flight from home you have also lost that of your mother's. Unfortunate child! you have no relations in the world but me!"--and she shed a flood of tears. Paul, pressing her in his arms, exclaimed, "Oh, my dear mother! since I have no relation in the world but you, I will love you all the more. But what a secret have you just disclosed to me! I now see the reason why Mademoiselle de la Tour has estranged herself so much from me for the last two months, and why she has determined to go to France. Ah! I perceive too well that she despises me!"

The hour of supper being arrived, we gathered round the table; but the different sensations with which we were agitated left us little inclination to eat, and the meal, if such it may be called, passed in silence. Virginia was the first to rise; she went out, and seated herself on the very spot where we now are. Paul hastened after her, and sat down by her side. Both of them, for some time, kept a profound silence. It was one of those delicious nights which are so common between the tropics, and to the beauty of which no pencil can do justice. The moon appeared in the midst of the firmament, surrounded by a curtain of clouds, which was gradually unfolded by her beams. Her light insensibly spread itself over the mountains of the island, and their distant peaks glistened with a silvery green. The winds were perfectly still. We heard among the woods, at the bottom of the valleys, and on the summits of the rocks, the piping cries and the soft notes of the birds, wantoning in their nests, and rejoicing in the brightness of the night and the serenity of the atmosphere. The hum of insects was heard in the grass. The stars sparkled in the heavens, and their lurid orbs were reflected, in trembling sparkles, from the tranquil bosom of the ocean. Virginia's eye wandered distractedly over its vast and gloomy horizon, distinguishable from the shore of the island only by the red fires in the fishing boats. She perceived at the entrance of the harbour a light and a shadow; these were the watchlight and the hull of the vessel in which she was to embark for Europe, and which, all ready for sea, lay at anchor, waiting for a breeze. Affected at this sight, she turned away her head, in order to hide her tears from Paul.

Madame de la Tour, Margaret, and I, were seated at a little distance, beneath the plantain-trees; and, owing to the stillness of the night, we distinctly heard their conversation, which I have not forgotten.

Paul said to her,--"You are going away from us, they tell me, in three days. You do not fear then to encounter the danger of the sea, at the sight of which you are so much terrified?" "I must perform my duty," answered Virginia, "by obeying my parent." "You leave us," resumed Paul, "for a distant relation, whom you have never seen." "Alas!" cried Virginia, "I would have remained here my whole life, but my mother would not have it so. My confessor, too, told me it was the will of God that I should go, and that life was a scene of trials!--and Oh! this is indeed a severe one."

"What!" exclaimed Paul, "you could find so many reasons for going, and not one for remaining here! Ah! there is one reason for your departure that you have not mentioned. Riches have great attractions. You will soon find in the new world to which you are going, another, to whom you will give the name of brother, which you bestow on me no more. You will choose that brother from amongst persons who are worthy of you by their birth, and by a fortune which I have not to offer.

But where can you go to be happier? On what shore will you land, and find it dearer to you than the spot which gave you birth?--and where will you form around you a society more delightful to you than this, by which you are so much accustomed? What will become of her, already advanced in years, when she no longer sees you at her side at table, in the house, in the walks, where she used to lean upon you? What will become of my mother, who loves you with the same affection? What shall I say to comfort them when I see them weeping for your absence? Cruel Virginia! I say nothing to you of myself; but what will become of me, when in the morning I shall no more see you; when the evening will come, and not reunite us?--when I shall gaze on these two palm trees, planted at our birth, and so long the witnesses of our mutual friendship? Ah! since your lot is changed,--since you seek in a far country other possessions than the fruits of my labour, let me go with you in the vessel in which you are about to embark. I will sustain your spirits in the midst of those tempests which terrify you so much even on shore. I will lay my head upon your bosom: I will warm your heart upon my own; and in France, where you are going in search of fortune and of grandeur, I will wait upon you as your slave. Happy only in your happiness, you will find me, in those palaces where I shall see you receiving the homage and adoration of all, rich and noble enough to make you the greatest of all sacrifices, by dying at your feet."

The violence of his emotions stopped his utterance, and we then heard Virginia, who, in a voice broken by sobs, uttered these words:--"It is for you that I go,--for you whom I see tired to death every day by the labour of sustaining two helpless families. If I have accepted this opportunity of becoming rich, it is only to return a thousand-fold the good which you have done us. Can any fortune be equal to your friendship? Why do you talk about your birth? Ah! if it were possible for me still to have a brother, should I make choice of any other than you? Oh, Paul, Paul! you are far dearer to me than a brother! How much has it cost me to repulse you from me! Help me to tear myself from what I value more than existence, till Heaven shall bless our union. But I will stay or go,--I will live or die,--dispose of me as you will. Unhappy that I am! I could have repelled your caresses; but I cannot support your affliction."

At these words Paul seized her in his arms, and, holding her pressed close to his bosom, cried, in a piercing tone, "I will go with her,--nothing shall ever part us."

We all ran towards him; and Madame de la Tour said to him, "My son, if you go, what will become of us?"

He, trembling, repeated after her the words,--"My son!--my son! You my mother!" cried he; "you, who would separate the brother from the sister! We have both been nourished at your bosom; we have both been reared upon your knees; we have learnt of you to love another; we have said so a thousand times; and now you would separate her from me!--you would send her to Europe, that inhospitable country which refused you an asylum, and to relations by whom you yourself were abandoned. You will tell me that I have no right over her, and that she is not my sister. She is everything to me;--my riches, my birth, my family,--all that I have! I know no other. We have had but one roof,--one cradle,--and we will have but one grave! If she goes, I will follow her. The governor will prevent me! Will he prevent me from flinging myself into the sea?--will he prevent me from following her by swimming? The sea cannot be more fatal to me than the land. Since I cannot live with her, at least I will die before her eyes, far from you. Inhuman mother!--woman without compassion!--may the ocean, to which you trust her, restore her to you no more! May the waves, rolling back our bodies amid the shingles of this beach, give you in the loss of your two children, an eternal subject of remorse!"

At these words, I seized him in my arms, for despair had deprived him of reason. His eyes sparkled with fire, the perspiration fell in great drops from his face; his knees trembled, and I felt his heart beat violently against his burning bosom.

Virginia, alarmed, said to him,--"Oh, my dear Paul, I call to witness the pleasures of our early age, your griefs and my own, and every thing that can for ever bind two unfortunate beings to each other, that if I remain at home, I will live but for you; that if I go, I will one day return to be yours. I call you all to witness;--you who have reared me from my infancy, who dispose of my life, and who see my tears. I swear by that Heaven which hears me, by the sea which I am going to pass, by the air I breathe, and which I never sullied by a falsehood."

As the sun softens and precipitates an icy rock from the summit of one of the Appenines, so the impetuous passions of the young man were subdued by the voice of her he loved. He bent his head, and a torrent of tears fell from his eyes. His mother, mingling her tears with his, held him in her arms, but was unable to speak. Madame de la Tour, half distracted, said to me, "I can bear this no longer. My heart is quite broken. This unfortunate voyage shall not take place. Do take my son home with you. Not one of us has had any rest the whole week."

I said to Paul, "My dear friend, your sister shall remain here. To-morrow we will talk to the governor about it; leave your family to take some rest, and come and pass the night with me. It is late; it is midnight; the southern cross is just above the horizon."

He suffered himself to be led away in silence; and, after a night of great agitation, he arose at break of day, and returned home.

But why should I continue any longer to you the recital of this history? There is but one aspect of human pleasure. Like the globe upon which we revolve, the fleeting course of life is but a day; and if one part of that day be visited by light, the other is thrown into darkness.

"My father," I answered, "finish, I conjure you, the history which you have begun in a manner so interesting. If the images of happiness are the most pleasing, those of misfortune are the more instructive. Tell me what became of the unhappy young man."

The first object beheld by Paul in his way home was the negro woman Mary, who, mounted on a rock, was earnestly looking towards the sea. As soon as he perceived her, he called to her from a distance,--"Where is Virginia?" Mary turned her head towards her young master, and began to weep. Paul, distracted, retracing his steps, ran to the harbour. He was there informed, that Virginia had embarked at the break of day, and that the vessel had immediately set sail, and was now out of sight. He instantly returned to the plantation, which he crossed without uttering a word.

Quite perpendicular as appears the wall of rocks behind us, those green platforms which separate their summits are so many stages, by means of which you may reach, through some difficult paths, that cone of sloping and inaccessible rocks, which is called The Thumb. At the foot of that cone is an extended slope of ground, covered with lofty trees, and so steep and elevated that it looks like a forest in the air, surrounded by tremendous precipices. The clouds, which are constantly attracted round the summit of the Thumb, supply innumerable rivulets, which fall to so great a depth in the valley situated on the other side of the mountain, that from this elevated point the sound of their cataracts cannot be heard. From that spot you can discern a considerable part of the island, diversified by precipices and mountain peaks, and amongst others, Peter-Booth, and the Three Breasts, with their valleys full of woods. You also command an extensive view of the ocean, and can even perceive the Isle of Bourbon, forty leagues to the westward. From the summit of that stupendous pile of rocks Paul caught sight of the vessel which was bearing away Virginia, and which now, ten leagues out at sea, appeared like a black spot in the midst of the ocean. He remained a great part of the day with his eyes fixed upon this object: when it had disappeared, he still fancied he beheld it; and when, at length, the traces which clung to his imagination were lost in the mists of the horizon, he seated himself on that wild point, forever beaten by the winds, which never cease to agitate the tops of the cabbage and gum trees, and the hoarse and moaning murmurs of which, similar to the distant sound of organs, inspire a profound melancholy. On this spot I found him, his head reclined on the rock, and his eyes fixed upon the ground. I had followed him from the earliest dawn, and, after much importunity, I prevailed on him to descend from the heights, and return to his family. I went home with him, where the first impulse of his mind, on seeing Madame de la Tour, was to reproach her bitterly for having deceived him. She told us that a favourable wind having sprung up at three o'clock in the morning, and the vessel being ready to sail, the governor, attended by some of his staff and the missionary, had come with a palanquin to fetch her daughter; and that, notwithstanding Virginia's objections, her own tears and entreaties, and the lamentations of Margaret, every body exclaiming all the time that it was for the general welfare, they had carried her away almost dying. "At least," cried Paul, "if I had bid her farewell, I should now be more calm. I would have said to her,--'Virginia, if, during the time we have lived together, one word may have escaped me which has offended you, before you leave me forever, tell me that you forgive me.' I would have said to her,--'Since I am destined to see you no more, farewell, my dear Virginia, farewell! Live far from me, contented and happy!'" When he saw that his mother and Madame de la Tour were weeping,--"You must now," said he, "seek some other hand to wipe away your tears;" and then, rushing out of the house, and groaning aloud, he wandered up and down the plantation. He hovered in particular about those spots which had been most endeared to Virginia. He said to the goats, and their little ones, which followed him, bleating,--"What do you want of me? You will see with me no more her who used to feed you with her own hand." He went to the bower called Virginia's Resting-place, and, as the birds flew around him, exclaimed, "Poor birds! you will fly no more to meet her who cherished you!"--and observing Fidele running backwards and forwards in search of her, he heaved a deep sigh, and cried,--"Ah! you will never find her again." At length he went and seated himself upon a rock where he had conversed with her the preceding evening; and at the sight of the ocean upon which he had seen the vessel disappear which had borne her away, his heart overflowed with anguish, and he wept bitterly.

We continually watched his movements, apprehensive of some fatal consequence from the violent agitation of his mind. His mother and Madame de la Tour conjured him, in the most tender manner, not to increase their affliction by his despair. At length the latter soothed his mind by lavishing upon him epithets calculated to awaken his hopes,--calling him her son, her dear son, her son-in-law, whom she destined for her daughter. She persuaded him to return home, and to take some food. He seated himself next to the place which used to be occupied by the companion of his childhood; and, as if she had still been present, he spoke to her, and made as though he would offer her whatever he knew as most agreeable to her taste: then, starting from this dream of fancy, he began to weep. For some days he employed himself in gathering together every thing which had belonged to Virginia, the last nosegays she had worn, the cocoa-shell from which she used to drink; and after kissing a thousand times these relics of his beloved, to him the most precious treasures which the world contained, he hid them in his bosom. Amber does not shed so sweet a perfume as the veriest trifles touched by those we love. At length, perceiving that the indulgence of his grief increased that of his mother and Madame de la Tour, and that the wants of the family demanded continual labour, he began, with the assistance of Domingo, to repair the damage done to the garden.

But, soon after, this young man, hitherto indifferent as a Creole to every thing that was passing in the world, begged of me to teach him to read and write, in order that he might correspond with Virginia. He afterwards wished to obtain a knowledge of geography, that he might form some idea of the country where she would disembark; and of history, that he might know something of the manners of the society in which she would be placed. The powerful sentiment of love, which directed his present studies, had already instructed him in agriculture, and in the art of laying out grounds with advantage and beauty. It must be admitted, that to the fond dreams of this restless and ardent passion, mankind are indebted for most of the arts and sciences, while its disappointments have given birth to philosophy, which teaches us to bear up under misfortune. Love, thus, the general link of all beings, becomes the great spring of society, by inciting us to knowledge as well as to pleasure.

Paul found little satisfaction in the study of geography, which, instead of describing the natural history of each country, gave only a view of its political divisions and boundaries. History, and especially modern history, interested him little more. He there saw only general and periodical evils, the causes of which he could not discover; wars without either motive or reason; uninteresting intrigues; with nations destitute of principle, and princes void of humanity. To this branch of reading he preferred romances, which, being chiefly occupied by the feelings and concerns of men, sometimes represented situations similar to his own. Thus, no book gave him so much pleasure as Telemachus, from the pictures it draws of pastoral life, and of the passions which are most natural to the human breast. He read aloud to his mother and Madame de la Tour, those parts which affected him most sensibly; but sometimes, touched by the most tender remembrances, his emotion would choke his utterance, and his eyes be filled with tears. He fancied he had found in Virginia the dignity and wisdom of Antiope, united to the misfortunes and the tenderness of Eucharis. With very different sensations he perused our fashionable novels, filled with licentious morals and maxims, and when he was informed that these works drew a tolerably faithful picture of European society, he trembled, and not without some appearance of reason, lest Virginia should become corrupted by it, and forget him.

More than a year and a half, indeed, passed away before Madame de la Tour received any tidings of her aunt or her daughter. During that period she only accidently heard that Virginia had safely arrived in France. At length, however, a vessel which stopped here on its way to the Indies brought a packet to Madame de la Tour, and a letter written by Virginia's own hand. Although this amiable and considerate girl had written in a guarded manner that she might not wound her mother's feelings, it appeared evident enough that she was unhappy. The letter painted so naturally her situation and her character, that I have retained it almost word for word.

"MY DEAR AND BELOVED MOTHER,

"I have already sent you several letters, written by my own hand, but having received no answer, I am afraid they have not reached you. I have better hopes for this, from the means I have now gained of sending you tidings of myself, and of hearing from you.

"I have shed many tears since our separation, I who never used to weep, but for the misfortunes of others! My aunt was much astonished, when, having, upon my arrival, inquired what accomplishments I possessed, I told her that I could neither read nor write. She asked me what then I had learnt, since I came into the world; and when I answered that I had been taught to take care of the household affairs, and to obey your will, she told me that I had received the education of a servant. The next day she placed me as a boarder in a great abbey near Paris, where I have masters of all kinds, who teach me, among other things, history, geography, grammar, mathematics, and riding on horseback. But I have so little capacity for all these sciences, that I fear I shall make but small progress with my masters. I feel that I am a very poor creature, with very little ability to learn what they teach. My aunt's kindness, however, does not decrease. She gives me new dresses every season; and she had placed two waiting women with me, who are dressed like fine ladies. She has made me take the title of countess; but has obliged me to renounce the name of LA TOUR, which is as dear to me as it is to you, from all you have told me of the sufferings my father endured in order to marry you. She has given me in place of your name that of your family, which is also dear to me, because it was your name when a girl. Seeing myself in so splendid a situation, I implored her to let me send you something to assist you. But how shall I repeat her answer! Yet you have desired me always to tell you the truth. She told me then that a little would be of no use to you, and that a great deal would only encumber you in the simple life you led. As you know I could not write, I endeavoured upon my arrival, to send you tidings of myself by another hand; but, finding no person here in whom I could place confidence, I applied night and day to learn to read and write, and Heaven, who saw my motive for learning, no doubt assisted my endeavours, for I succeeded in both in a short time. I entrusted my first letters to some of the ladies here, who, I have reason to think, carried them to my aunt. This time I have recourse to a boarder, who is my friend. I send you her direction, by means of which I shall receive your answer.

My aunt has forbid me holding any correspondence whatever, with any one, lest, she says, it should occasion an obstacle to the great views she has for my advantage. No person is allowed to see me at the grate but herself, and an old nobleman, one of her friends, who, she says is much pleased with me. I am sure I am not at all so with him, nor should I, even if it were possible for me to be pleased with any one at present.

"I live in all the splendour of affluence, and have not a sous at my disposal. They say I might make an improper use of money. Even my clothes belong to my femmes de chambre, who quarrel about them before I have left them off. In the midst of riches I am poorer than when I lived with you; for I have nothing to give away. When I found that the great accomplishments they taught me would not procure me the power of doing the smallest good, I had recourse to my needle, of which happily you had taught me the use. I send several pairs of stockings of my own making for you and my mamma Margaret, a cap for Domingo, and one of my red handkerchiefs for Mary. I also send with this packet some kernels, and seeds of various kinds of fruits which I gathered in the abbey park during my hours of recreation. I have also sent a few seeds of violets, daisies, buttercups, poppies and scabious, which I picked up in the fields. There are much more beautiful flowers in the meadows of this country than in ours, but nobody cares for them. I am sure that you and my mamma Margaret will be better pleased with this bag of seeds, than you were with the bag of piastres, which was the cause of our separation and of my tears. It will give me great delight if you should one day see apple trees growing by the side of our plantains, and elms blending their foliage with that of our cocoa trees. You will fancy yourself in Normandy, which you love so much.

"You desired me to relate to you my joys and my griefs. I have no joys far from you. As far as my griefs, I endeavour to soothe them by reflecting that I am in the situation in which it was the will of God that you should place me. But my greatest affliction is, that no one here speaks to me of you, and that I cannot speak of you to any one. My femmes de chambre, or rather those of my aunt, for they belong more to her than to me, told me the other day, when I wished to turn the conversation upon the objects most dear to me: 'Remember, mademoiselle, that you are a French woman, and must forget that land of savages.' Ah! sooner will I forget myself, than forget the spot on which I was born and where you dwell! It is this country which is to me a land of savages, for I live alone, having no one to whom I can impart those feelings of tenderness for you which I shall bear with me to the grave. I am,

"My dearest and beloved mother,

"Your affectionate and dutiful daughter,

"VIRGINIE DE LA TOUR."

"I recommend to your goodness Mary and Domingo, who took so much care of my infancy; caress Fidele for me, who found me in the wood."

Paul was astonished that Virginia had not said one word of him,--she, who had not forgotten even the house-dog. But he was not aware that, however long a woman's letter may be, she never fails to leave her dearest sentiments for the end.

In a postscript, Virginia particularly recommended to Paul's attention two kinds of seed,--those of the violet and the scabious. She gave him some instructions upon the natural characters of these flowers, and the spots most proper for their cultivation. "The violet," she said, "produces a little flower of a dark purple colour, which delights to conceal itself beneath the bushes; but it is soon discovered by its wide-spreading perfume." She desired that these seeds might be sown by the border of the fountain, at the foot of her cocoa-tree. "The scabious," she added, "produces a beautiful flower of a pale blue, and a black ground spotted with white. You might fancy it was in mourning; and for this reason it is also called the widow's flower. It grows best in bleak spots, beaten by the winds." She begged him to sow this upon the rock where she had spoken to him at night for the last time, and that, in remembrance of her, he would henceforth give it the name of the Rock of Adieus.

She had put these seeds into a little purse, the tissue of which was exceedingly simple; but which appeared above all price to Paul, when he saw on it a P and a V entwined together, and knew that the beautiful hair which formed the cypher was the hair of Virginia.

The whole family listened with tears to the reading of the letter of this amiable and virtuous girl. Her mother answered it in the name of the little society, desiring her to remain or to return as she thought proper; and assuring her, that happiness had left their dwelling since her departure, and that, for herself, she was inconsolable.

Paul also sent her a very long letter, in which he assured her that he would arrange the garden in a manner agreeable to her taste, and mingle together in it the plants of Europe with those of Africa, as she had blended their initials together in her work. He sent her some fruit from the cocoa-trees of the fountain, now arrived at maturity telling her, that he would not add any of the other productions of the island, that the desire of seeing them again might hasten her return. He conjured her to comply as soon as possible with the ardent wishes of her family, and above all, with his own, since he could never hereafter taste happiness away from her.

Paul sowed with a careful hand the European seeds, particularly the violet and the scabious, the flowers of which seemed to bear some analogy to the character and present situation of Virginia, by whom they had been so especially recommended; but either they were dried up in the voyage, or the climate of this part of the world is unfavourable to their growth, for a very small number of them even came up, and not one arrived at full perfection.

In the meantime, envy, which ever comes to embitter human happiness, particularly in the French colonies, spread some reports in the island which gave Paul much uneasiness. The passengers in the vessel which brought Virginia's letter, asserted that she was upon the point of being married, and named the nobleman of the court to whom she was engaged. Some even went so far as to declare that the union had already taken place, and that they themselves had witnessed the ceremony. Paul at first despised the report, brought by a merchant vessel, as he knew that they often spread erroneous intelligence in their passage; but some of the inhabitants of the island, with malignant pity, affecting to bewail the event, he was soon led to attach some degree of belief to this cruel intelligence. Besides, in some of the novels he had lately read, he had seen that perfidy was treated as a subject of pleasantry; and knowing that these books contained pretty faithful representations of European manners, he feared that the heart of Virginia was corrupted, and had forgotten its former engagements. Thus his new acquirements had already only served to render him more miserable; and his apprehensions were much increased by the circumstance, that though several ships touched here from Europe, within the six months immediately following the arrival of her letter, not one of them brought any tidings of Virginia.

This unfortunate young man, with a heart torn by the most cruel agitation, often came to visit me, in the hope of confirming or banishing his uneasiness, by my experience of the world.

I live, as I have already told you, a league and a half from this point, upon the banks of a little river which glides along the Sloping Mountain: there I lead a solitary life, without wife, children, or slaves.

After having enjoyed, and lost the rare felicity of living with a congenial mind, the state of life which appears the least wretched is doubtless that of solitude. Every man who has much cause of complaint against his fellow-creatures seeks to be alone. It is also remarkable that all those nations which have been brought to wretchedness by their opinions, their manners, or their forms of government, have produced numerous classes of citizens altogether devoted to solitude and celibacy. Such were the Egyptians in their decline, and the Greeks of the Lower Empire; and such in our days are the Indians, the Chinese, the modern Greeks, the Italians, and the greater part of the eastern and southern nations of Europe. Solitude, by removing men from the miseries which follow in the train of social intercourse, brings them in some degree back to the unsophisticated enjoyment of nature. In the midst of modern society, broken up by innumerable prejudices, the mind is in a constant turmoil of agitation. It is incessantly revolving in itself a thousand tumultuous and contradictory opinions, by which the members of an ambitious and miserable circle seek to raise themselves above each other. But in solitude the soul lays aside the morbid illusions which troubled her, and resumes the pure consciousness of herself, of nature, and of its Author, as the muddy water of a torrent which has ravaged the plains, coming to rest, and diffusing itself over some low grounds out of its course, deposits there the slime it has taken up, and, resuming its wonted transparency, reflects, with its own shores, the verdure of the earth and the light of heaven. Thus does solitude recruit the powers of the body as well as those of the mind. It is among hermits that are found the men who carry human existence to its extreme limits; such are the Bramins of India. In brief, I consider solitude so necessary to happiness, even in the world itself, that it appears to me impossible to derive lasting pleasure from any pursuit whatever, or to regulate our conduct by any pursuit whatever, or to regulate our conduct by any stable principle, if we do not create for ourselves a mental void, whence our own views rarely emerge, and into which the opinions of others never enter. I do not mean to say that man ought to live absolutely alone; he is connected by his necessities with all mankind; his labours are due to man: and he owes something too to the rest of nature. But, as God has given to each of us organs perfectly adapted to the elements of the globe on which we live,--feet for the soil, lungs for the air, eyes for the light, without the power of changing the use of any of these faculties, he has reserved for himself, as the Author of life, that which is its chief organ,--the heart.

I thus passed my days far from mankind, whom I wished to serve, and by whom I have been persecuted. After having travelled over many countries of Europe, and some parts of America and Africa, I at length pitched my tent in this thinly-peopled island, allured by its mild climate and its solitudes. A cottage which I built in the woods, at the foot of a tree, a little field which I cleared with my own hands, a river which glides before my door, suffice for my wants and for my pleasures. I blend with these enjoyments the perusal of some chosen books, which teach me to become better. They make that world, which I have abandoned, still contribute something to my happiness. They lay before me pictures of those passions which render its inhabitants so miserable; and in the comparison I am thus led to make between their lot and my own, I feel a kind of negative enjoyment. Like a man saved from shipwreck, and thrown upon a rock, I contemplate, from my solitude, the storms which rage through the rest of the world; and my repose seems more profound from the distant sound of the tempest. As men have ceased to fall in my way, I no longer view them with aversion; I only pity them. If I sometimes fall in with an unfortunate being, I try to help him by my counsels, as a passer-by on the brink of a torrent extends his hand to save a wretch from drowning. But I have hardly ever found any but the innocent attentive to my voice. Nature calls the majority of men to her in vain. Each of them forms an image of her for himself, and invests her with his own passions. He pursues during the whole of his life this vain phantom, which leads him astray; and he afterwards complains to Heaven of the misfortunes which he has thus created for himself. Among the many children of misfortune whom I have endeavoured to lead back to the enjoyments of nature, I have not found one but was intoxicated with his own miseries. They have listened to me at first with attention, in the hope that I could teach them how to acquire glory or fortune, but when they found that I only wished to instruct them how to dispense with these chimeras, their attention has been converted into pity, because I did not prize their miserable happiness. They blamed my solitary life; they alleged that they alone were useful to men, and they endeavoured to draw me into their vortex. But if I communicate with all, I lay myself open to none. It is often sufficient for me to serve as a lesson to myself. In my present tranquillity, I pass in review the agitating pursuits of my past life, to which I formerly attached so much value,--patronage, fortune, reputation, pleasure, and the opinions which are ever at strife over all the earth. I compare the men whom I have seen disputing furiously over these vanities, and who are no more, to the tiny waves of my rivulet, which break in foam against its rocky bed, and disappear, never to return. As for me, I suffer myself to float calmly down the stream of time to the shoreless ocean of futurity; while, in the contemplation of the present harmony of nature, I elevate my soul towards its supreme Author, and hope for a more happy lot in another state of existence.

Although you cannot descry from my hermitage, situated in the midst of a forest, that immense variety of objects which this elevated spot presents, the grounds are disposed with peculiar beauty, at least to one who, like me, prefers the seclusion of a home scene to great and extensive prospects. The river which glides before my door passes in a straight line across the woods, looking like a long canal shaded by all kinds of trees. Among them are the gum tree, the ebony tree, and that which is here called bois de pomme, with olive and cinnamon-wood trees; while in some parts the cabbage-palm trees raise their naked stems more than a hundred feet high, their summits crowned with a cluster of leaves, and towering above the woods like one forest piled upon another. Lianas, of various foliage, intertwining themselves among the trees, form, here, arcades of foliage, there, long canopies of verdure. Most of these trees shed aromatic odours so powerful, that the garments of a traveller, who has passed through the forest, often retain for hours the most delicious fragrance. In the season when they produce their lavish blossoms, they appear as if half-covered with snow. Towards the end of summer, various kinds of foreign birds hasten, impelled by some inexplicable instinct, from unknown regions on the other side of immense oceans, to feed upon the grain and other vegetable productions of the island; and the brilliancy of their plumage forms a striking contrast to the more sombre tints of the foliage embrowned by the sun. Among these are various kinds of parroquets, and the blue pigeon, called here the pigeon of Holland. Monkeys, the domestic inhabitants of our forests, sport upon the dark branches of the trees, from which they are easily distinguished by their gray and greenish skin, and their black visages. Some hang, suspended by the tail, and swing themselves in air; others leap from branch to branch, bearing their young in their arms. The murderous gun has never affrighted these peaceful children of nature. You hear nothing but sounds of joy,--the warblings and unknown notes of birds from the countries of the south, repeated from a distance by the echoes of the forest. The river, which pours, in foaming eddies, over a bed of rocks, through the midst of the woods, reflects here and there upon its limpid waters their venerable masses of verdure and of shade, along with the sports of their happy inhabitants. About a thousand paces from thence it forms several cascades, clear as crystal in their fall, but broken at the bottom into frothy surges. Innumerable confused sounds issue from these watery tumults, which, borne by the winds across the forest, now sink in distance, now all at once swell out, booming on the ear like the bells of a cathedral. The air, kept ever in motion by the running water, preserves upon the banks of the river, amid all the summer heats, a freshness and verdure rarely found in this island, even on the summits of the mountains.

At some distance from this place is a rock, placed far enough from the cascade to prevent the ear from being deafened with the noise of its waters, and sufficiently near for the enjoyment of seeing it, of feeling its coolness, and hearing its gentle murmurs. Thither, amidst the heats of summer, Madame de la Tour, Margaret, Virginia, Paul, and myself, sometimes repaired, to dine beneath the shadow of this rock. Virginia, who always, in her most ordinary actions, was mindful of the good of others, never ate of any fruit in the fields without planting the seed or kernel in the ground. "From this," said she, "trees will come, which will yield their fruit to some traveller, or at least to some bird." One day, having eaten of the papaw fruit at the foot of that rock, she planted the seeds on the spot. Soon after, several papaw trees sprang up, among which was one with female blossoms, that is to say, a fruit-bearing tree. This tree, at the time of Virginia's departure, was scarcely as high as her knee; but, as it is a plant of rapid growth, in the course of two years it had gained the height of twenty feet, and the upper part of its stem was encircled by several rows of ripe fruit. Paul, wandering accidentally to the spot, was struck with delight at seeing this lofty tree, which had been planted by his beloved; but the emotion was transient, and instantly gave place to a deep melancholy, at this evidence of her long absence. The objects which are habitually before us do not bring to our minds an adequate idea of the rapidity of life; they decline insensibly with ourselves: but it is those we behold again, that most powerfully impress us with a feeling of the swiftness with which the tide of life flows on. Paul was no less over-whelmed and affected at the sight of this great papaw tree, loaded with fruit, than is the traveller when, after a long absence from his own country, he finds his contemporaries no more, but their children, whom he left at the breast, themselves now become fathers of families. Paul sometimes thought of cutting down the tree, which recalled too sensibly the distracting remembrance of Virginia's prolonged absence. At other times, contemplating it as a monument of her benevolence, he kissed its trunk, and apostrophized it in terms of the most passionate regret. Indeed, I have myself gazed upon it with more emotion and more veneration than upon the triumphal arches of Rome. May nature, which every day destroys the monuments of kingly ambition, multiply in our forests those which testify the beneficence of a poor young girl!

At the foot of this papaw tree I was always sure to meet with Paul when he came into our neighbourhood. One day, I found him there absorbed in melancholy and a conversation took place between us, which I will relate to you, if I do not weary you too much by my long digressions; they are perhaps pardonable to my age and to my last friendships. I will relate it to you in the form of a dialogue, that you may form some idea of the natural good sense of this young man. You will easily distinguish the speakers, from the character of his questions and of my answers.

Paul.--I am very unhappy. Mademoiselle de la Tour has now been gone two years and eight months and a half. She is rich, and I am poor; she has forgotten me. I have a great mind to follow her. I will go to France; I will serve the king; I will make my fortune; and then Mademoiselle de la Tour's aunt will bestow her niece upon me when I shall have become a great lord.

The Old Man.--But, my dear friend, have not you told me that you are not of noble birth?

Paul.--My mother has told me so; but, as for myself, I know not what noble birth means. I never perceived that I had less than others, or that others had more than I.

The Old Man.--Obscure birth, in France, shuts every door of access to great employments; nor can you even be received among any distinguished body of men, if you labour under this disadvantage.

Paul.--You have often told me that it was one source of the greatness of France that her humblest subject might attain the highest honours; and you have cited to me many instances of celebrated men who, born in a mean condition, had conferred honour upon their country. It was your wish, then, by concealing the truth to stimulate my ardour?

The Old Man.--Never, my son, would I lower it. I told you the truth with regard to the past; but now, every thing has undergone a great change. Every thing in France is now to be obtained by interest alone; every place and employment is now become as it were the patrimony of a small number of families, or is divided among public bodies. The king is a sun, and the nobles and great corporate bodies surround him like so many clouds; it is almost impossible for any of his rays to reach you. Formerly, under less exclusive administrations, such phenomena have been seen. Then talents and merit showed themselves every where, as newly cleared lands are always loaded with abundance. But great kings, who can really form a just estimate of men, and choose them with judgment, are rare. The ordinary race of monarchs allow themselves to be guided by the nobles and people who surround them.

Paul.--But perhaps I shall find one of these nobles to protect me.

The Old Man.--To gain the protection of the great you must lend yourself to their ambition, and administer to their pleasures. You would never succeed; for, in addition to your obscure birth, you have too much integrity.

Paul.--But I will perform such courageous actions, I will be so faithful to my word, so exact in the performance of my duties, so zealous and so constant in my friendships, that I will render myself worthy to be adopted by some one of them. In the ancient histories, you have made me read, I have seen many examples of such adoptions.

The Old Man.--Oh, my young friend! among the Greeks and Romans, even in their decline, the nobles had some respect for virtue; but out of all the immense number of men, sprung from the mass of the people, in France, who have signalized themselves in every possible manner, I do not recollect a single instance of one being adopted by any great family. If it were not for our kings, virtue, in our country, would be eternally condemned as plebeian. As I said before, the monarch sometimes, when he perceives it, renders to it due honour; but in the present day, the distinctions which should be bestowed on merit are generally to be obtained by money alone.

Paul.--If I cannot find a nobleman to adopt me, I will seek to please some public body. I will espouse its interests and its opinions: I will make myself beloved by it.

The Old Man.--You will act then like other men?--you will renounce your conscience to obtain a fortune?

Paul.--Oh no! I will never lend myself to any thing but the truth.

The Old Man.--Instead of making yourself beloved, you would become an object of dislike. Besides, public bodies have never taken much interest in the discovery of truth. All opinions are nearly alike to ambitious men, provided only that they themselves can gain their ends.

Paul.--How unfortunate I am! Every thing bars my progress. I am condemned to pass my life in ignoble toil, far from Virginia.

As he said this he sighed deeply.

The Old Man.--Let God be your patron, and mankind the public body you would serve. Be constantly attached to them both. Families, corporations, nations and kings have, all of them, their prejudices and their passions; it is often necessary to serve them by the practice of vice: God and mankind at large require only the exercise of the virtues.

But why do you wish to be distinguished from other men? It is hardly a natural sentiment, for, if all men possessed it, every one would be at constant strife with his neighbour. Be satisfied with fulfilling your duty in the station in which Providence has placed you; be grateful for your lot, which permits you to enjoy the blessing of a quiet conscience, and which does not compel you, like the great, to let your happiness rest on the opinion of the little, or, like the little, to cringe to the great, in order to obtain the means of existence. You are now placed in a country and a condition in which you are not reduced to deceive or flatter any one, or debase yourself, as the greater part of those who seek their fortune in Europe are obliged to do; in which the exercise of no virtue is forbidden you; in which you may be, with impunity, good, sincere, well-informed, patient, temperate, chaste, indulgent to others' faults, pious and no shaft of ridicule be aimed at you to destroy your wisdom, as yet only in its bud. Heaven has given you liberty, health, a good conscience, and friends; kings themselves, whose favour you desire, are not so happy.

Paul.--Ah! I only want to have Virginia with me: without her I have nothing,--with her, I should possess all my desire. She alone is to me birth, glory, and fortune. But, since her relations will only give her to some one with a great name, I will study. By the aid of study and of books, learning and celebrity are to be attained. I will become a man of science: I will render my knowledge useful to the service of my country, without injuring any one, or owning dependence on any one. I will become celebrated, and my glory shall be achieved only by myself.

The Old Man.--My son, talents are a gift yet more rare than either birth or riches, and undoubtedly they are a greater good than either, since they can never be taken away from us, and that they obtain for us every where public esteem. But they may be said to be worth all that they cost us. They are seldom acquired but by every species of privation, by the possession of exquisite sensibility, which often produces inward unhappiness, and which exposes us without to the malice and persecutions of our contemporaries. The lawyer envies not, in France, the glory of the soldier, nor does the soldier envy that of the naval officer; but they will all oppose you, and bar your progress to distinction, because your assumption of superior ability will wound the self-love of them all. You say that you will do good to men; but recollect, that he who makes the earth produce a single ear of corn more, renders them a greater service than he who writes a book.

Paul.--Oh! she, then, who planted this papaw tree, has made a more useful and more grateful present to the inhabitants of these forests than if she had given them a whole library.

So saying, he threw his arms around the tree, and kissed it with transport.

The Old Man.--The best of books,--that which preaches nothing but equality, brotherly love, charity, and peace,--the Gospel, has served as a pretext, during many centuries, for Europeans to let loose all their fury. How many tyrannies, both public and private, are still practised in its name on the face of the earth! After this, who will dare to flatter himself that any thing he can write will be of service to his fellow men? Remember the fate of most of the philosophers who have preached to them wisdom. Homer, who clothes it in such noble verse, asked for alms all his life. Socrates, whose conversation and example gave such admirable lessons to the Athenians, was sentenced by them to be poisoned. His sublime disciple, Plato was delivered over to slavery by the order of the very prince who protected him; and, before them, Pythagoras, whose humanity extended even to animals, was burned alive by the Crotoniates. What do I say?--many even of these illustrious names have descended to us disfigured by some traits of satire by which they became characterized, human ingratitude taking pleasure in thus recognising them; and if, in the crowd, the glory of some names is come down to us without spot or blemish, we shall find that they who have borne them have lived far from the society of their contemporaries; like those statues which are found entire beneath the soil in Greece and Italy, and which, by being hidden in the bosom of the earth, have escaped uninjured, from the fury of the barbarians.

You see, then, that to acquire the glory which a turbulent literary career can give you, you must not only be virtuous, but ready, if necessary, to sacrifice life itself. But, after all, do not fancy that the great in France trouble themselves about such glory as this. Little do they care for literary men, whose knowledge brings them neither honours, nor power, nor even admission at court. Persecution, it is true, is rarely practised in this age, because it is habitually indifferent to every thing except wealth and luxury; but knowledge and virtue no longer lead to distinction, since every thing in the state is to be purchased with money. Formerly, men of letters were certain of reward by some place in the church, the magistracy, or the administration; now they are considered good for nothing but to write books. But this fruit of their minds, little valued by the world at large, is still worthy of its celestial origin. For these books is reserved the privilege of shedding lustre on obscure virtue, of consoling the unhappy, of enlightening nations, and of telling the truth even to kings. This is, unquestionably, the most august commission with which Heaven can honour a mortal upon this earth. Where is the author who would not be consoled for the injustice or contempt of those who are the dispensers of the ordinary gifts of fortune, when he reflects that his work may pass from age to age, from nation to nation, opposing a barrier to error and to tyranny; and that, from amidst the obscurity in which he has lived, there will shine forth a glory which will efface that of the common herd of monarchs, the monuments of whose deeds perish in oblivion, notwithstanding the flatterers who erect and magnify them?

Paul.--Ah! I am only covetous of glory to bestow it on Virginia, and render her dear to the whole world. But can you, who know so much, tell me whether we shall ever be married? I should like to be a very learned man, if only for the sake of knowing what will come to pass.

The Old Man.--Who would live, my son, if the future were revealed to him?--when a single anticipated misfortune gives us so much useless uneasiness--when the foreknowledge of one certain calamity is enough to embitter every day that precedes it! It is better not to pry too curiously, even into the things which surround us. Heaven, which has given us the power of reflection to foresee our necessities, gave us also those very necessities to set limits to its exercise.

Paul.--You tell me that with money people in Europe acquire dignities and honours. I will go, then, to enrich myself in Bengal, and afterwards proceed to Paris, and marry Virginia. I will embark at once.

The Old Man.--What! would you leave her mother and yours?

Paul.--Why, you yourself have advised my going to the Indies.

The Old Man.--Virginia was then here; but you are now the only means of support both of her mother and of your own.

Paul.--Virginia will assist them by means of her rich relation.

The Old Man.--The rich care little for those, from whom no honour is reflected upon themselves in the world. Many of them have relations much more to be pitied than Madame de la Tour, who, for want of their assistance, sacrifice their liberty for bread, and pass their lives immured within the walls of a convent.

Paul.--Oh, what a country is Europe! Virginia must come back here. What need has she of a rich relation? She was so happy in these huts; she looked so beautiful and so well dressed with a red handkerchief or a few flowers around her head! Return, Virginia! leave your sumptuous mansions and your grandeur, and come back to these rocks,--to the shade of these woods and of our cocoa trees. Alas! you are perhaps even now unhappy!"--and he began to shed tears. "My father," continued he, "hide nothing from me; if you cannot tell me whether I shall marry Virginia, tell me at least if she loves me still, surrounded as she is by noblemen who speak to the king, and who go to see her."

The Old Man.--Oh, my dear friend! I am sure, for many reasons, that she loves you; but above all, because she is virtuous. At these words he threw himself on my neck in a transport of joy.

Paul.--But do you think that the women of Europe are false, as they are represented in the comedies and books which you have lent me?

The Old Man.--Women are false in those countries where men are tyrants. Violence always engenders a disposition to deceive.

Paul.--In what way can men tyrannize over women?

The Old Man.--In giving them in marriage without consulting their inclinations;--in uniting a young girl to an old man, or a woman of sensibility to a frigid and indifferent husband.

Paul.--Why not join together those who are suited to each other,--the young to the young, and lovers to those they love?

The Old Man.--Because few young men in France have property enough to support them when they are married, and cannot acquire it till the greater part of their life is passed. While young, they seduce the wives of others, and when they are old, they cannot secure the affections of their own. At first, they themselves are deceivers: and afterwards, they are deceived in their turn. This is one of the reactions of that eternal justice, by which the world is governed; an excess on one side is sure to be balanced by one on the other. Thus, the greater part of Europeans pass their lives in this twofold irregularity, which increases everywhere in the same proportion that wealth is accumulated in the hands of a few individuals. Society is like a garden, where shrubs cannot grow if they are overshadowed by lofty trees; but there is this wide difference between them,--that the beauty of a garden may result from the admixture of a small number of forest trees, while the prosperity of a state depends on the multitude and equality of its citizens, and not on a small number of very rich men.

Paul.--But where is the necessity of being rich in order to marry?

The Old Man.--In order to pass through life in abundance, without being obliged to work.

Paul.--But why not work? I am sure I work hard enough.

The Old Man.--In Europe, working with your hands is considered a degradation; it is compared to the labour performed by a machine. The occupation of cultivating the earth is the most despised of all. Even an artisan is held in more estimation than a peasant.

Paul.--What! do you mean to say that the art which furnishes food for mankind is despised in Europe? I hardly understand you.

The Old Man.--Oh! it is impossible for a person educated according to nature to form an idea of the depraved state of society. It is easy to form a precise notion of order, but not of disorder. Beauty, virtue, happiness, have all their defined proportions; deformity, vice, and misery have none.

Paul.--The rich then are always very happy! They meet with no obstacles to the fulfilment of their wishes, and they can lavish happiness on those whom they love.

The Old Man.--Far from it, my son! They are, for the most part satiated with pleasure, for this very reason,--that it costs them no trouble. Have you never yourself experienced how much the pleasure of repose is increased by fatigue; that of eating, by hunger; or that of drinking, by thirst? The pleasure also of loving and being loved is only to be acquired by innumerable privations and sacrifices. Wealth, by anticipating all their necessities, deprives its possessors of all these pleasures. To this ennui, consequent upon satiety, may also be added the pride which springs from their opulence, and which is wounded by the most trifling privation, when the greatest enjoyments have ceased to charm. The perfume of a thousand roses gives pleasure but for a moment; but the pain occasioned by a single thorn endures long after the infliction of the wound. A single evil in the midst of their pleasures is to the rich like a thorn among flowers; to the poor, on the contrary, one pleasure amidst all their troubles is a flower among a wilderness of thorns; they have a most lively enjoyment of it. The effect of every thing is increased by contrast; nature has balanced all things. Which condition, after all, do you consider preferable,--to have scarcely any thing to hope, and every thing to fear, or to have every thing to hope and nothing to fear? The former condition is that of the rich, the latter, that of the poor. But either of these extremes is with difficulty supported by man, whose happiness consists in a middle station of life, in union with virtue.

Paul.--What do you understand by virtue?

The Old Man.--To you, my son, who support your family by your labour, it need hardly be defined. Virtue consists in endeavouring to do all the good we can to others, with an ultimate intention of pleasing God alone.

Paul.--Oh! how virtuous, then, is Virginia! Virtue led her to seek for riches, that she might practise benevolence. Virtue induced her to quit this island, and virtue will bring her back to it.

The idea of her speedy return firing the imagination of this young man, all his anxieties suddenly vanished. Virginia, he was persuaded, had not written, because she would soon arrive. It took so little time to come from Europe with a fair wind! Then he enumerated the vessels which had made this passage of four thousand five hundred leagues in less than three months; and perhaps the vessel in which Virginia had embarked might not be more than two. Ship-builders were now so ingenious, and sailors were so expert! He then talked to me of the arrangements he intended to make for her reception, of the new house he would build for her, and of the pleasures and surprises which he would contrive for her every day, when she was his wife. His wife! The idea filled him with ecstasy. "At least, my dear father," said he, "you shall then do no more work than you please. As Virginia will be rich, we shall have plenty of negroes, and they shall work for you. You shall always live with us, and have no other care than to amuse yourself and be happy;"--and, his heart throbbing with joy, he flew to communicate these exquisite anticipations to his family.

In a short time, however, these enchanting hopes were succeeded by the most cruel apprehensions. It is always the effect of violent passions to throw the soul into opposite extremes. Paul returned the next day to my dwelling, overwhelmed with melancholy, and said to me,--"I hear nothing from Virginia. Had she left Europe she would have written me word of her departure. Ah! the reports which I have heard concerning her are but too well founded. Her aunt has married her to some great lord. She, like others, has been undone by the love of riches. In those books which paint women so well, virtue is treated but as a subject of romance. If Virginia had been virtuous, she would never have forsaken her mother and me. I do nothing but think of her, and she has forgotten me. I am wretched, and she is diverting herself. The thought distracts me; I cannot bear myself! Would to Heaven that war were declared in India! I would go there and die."

"My son," I answered, "that courage which prompts us to court death is but the courage of a moment, and is often excited by the vain applause of men, or by the hopes of posthumous renown. There is another description of courage, rarer and more necessary, which enables us to support, without witness and without applause, the vexations of life; this virtue is patience. Relying for support, not upon the opinions of others, or the impulse of the passions, but upon the will of God, patience is the courage of virtue."

"Ah!" cried he, "I am then without virtue! Every thing overwhelms me and drives me to despair."--"Equal, constant, and invariable virtue," I replied, "belongs not to man. In the midst of the many passions which agitate us, our reason is disordered and obscured: but there is an everburning lamp, at which we can rekindle its flame; and that is, literature.

"Literature, my dear son, is the gift of Heaven, a ray of that wisdom by which the universe is governed, and which man, inspired by a celestial intelligence, has drawn down to earth. Like the rays of the sun, it enlightens us, it rejoices us, it warms us with a heavenly flame, and seems, in some sort, like the element of fire, to bend all nature to our use. By its means we are enabled to bring around us all things, all places, all men, and all times. It assists us to regulate our manners and our life. By its aid, too, our passions are calmed, vice is suppressed, and virtue encouraged by the memorable examples of great and good men which it has handed down to us, and whose time-honoured images it ever brings before our eyes. Literature is a daughter of Heaven who has descended upon earth to soften and to charm away all the evils of the human race. The greatest writers have ever appeared in the worst times,--in times in which society can hardly be held together,--the times of barbarism and every species of depravity. My son, literature has consoled an infinite number of men more unhappy than yourself: Xenophon, banished from his country after having saved to her ten thousand of her sons; Scipio Africanus, wearied to death by the calumnies of the Romans; Lucullus, tormented by their cabals; and Catinat, by the ingratitude of a court. The Greeks, with their never-failing ingenuity, assigned to each of the Muses a portion of the great circle of human intelligence for her especial superintendence; we ought in the same manner, to give up to them the regulation of our passions, to bring them under proper restraint. Literature in this imaginative guise, would thus fulfil, in relation to the powers of the soul, the same functions as the Hours, who yoked and conducted the chariot of the Sun.

"Have recourse to your books, then, my son. The wise who have written before our days are travellers who have preceded us in the paths of misfortune, and who stretch out a friendly hand towards us, and invite us to join in their society, when we are abandoned by every thing else. A good book is a good friend."

"Ah!" cried Paul, "I stood in no need of books when Virginia was here, and she had studied as little as myself; but when she looked at me, and called me her friend, I could not feel unhappy."

"Undoubtedly," said I, "there is no friend so agreeable as a mistress by whom we are beloved. There is, moreover, in woman a liveliness and gaiety, which powerfully tend to dissipate the melancholy feelings of a man; her presence drives away the dark phantoms of imagination produced by over-reflection. Upon her countenance sit soft attraction and tender confidence. What joy is not heightened when it is shared by her? What brow is not unbent by her smiles? What anger can resist her tears? Virginia will return with more philosophy than you, and will be quite surprised to find the garden so unfinished;--she who could think of its embellishments in spite of all the persecutions of her aunt, and when far from her mother and from you."

The idea of Virginia's speedy return reanimated the drooping spirits of her lover, and he resumed his rural occupations, happy amidst his toils, in the reflection that they would soon find a termination so dear to the wishes of his heart.

One morning, at break of day, (it was the 24th of December, 1744,) Paul, when he arose, perceived a white flag hoisted upon the Mountain of Discovery. This flag he knew to be the signal of a vessel descried at sea. He instantly flew to the town to learn if this vessel brought any tidings of Virginia, and waited there till the return of the pilot, who was gone, according to custom, to board the ship. The pilot did not return till the evening, when he brought the governor information that the signalled vessel was the Saint-Geran, of seven hundred tons burthen, and commanded by a captain of the name of Aubin; that she was now four leagues out at sea, but would probably anchor at Port Louis the following afternoon, if the wind became fair: at present there was a calm. The pilot then handed to the governor a number of letters which the Saint-Geran had brought from France, among which was one addressed to Madame de la Tour, in the hand-writing of Virginia. Paul seized upon the letter, kissed it with transport, and placing it in his bosom, flew to the plantation. No sooner did he perceive from a distance the family, who were awaiting his return upon the rock of Adieus than he waved the letter aloft in the air, without being able to utter a word. No sooner was the seal broken, than they all crowded round Madame de la Tour, to hear the letter read. Virginia informed her mother that she had experienced much ill-usage from her aunt, who, after having in vain urged her to a marriage against her inclination, had disinherited her, and had sent her back at a time when she would probably reach the Mauritius during the hurricane season. In vain, she added, had she endeavoured to soften her aunt, by representing what she owed to her mother, and to her early habits; she was treated as a romantic girl, whose head had been turned by novels. She could now only think of the joy of again seeing and embracing her beloved family, and would have gratified her ardent desire at once, by landing in the pilot's boat, if the captain had allowed her: but that he had objected, on account of the distance, and of a heavy swell, which, notwithstanding the calm, reigned in the open sea.

As soon as the letter was finished, the whole of the family, transported with joy, repeatedly exclaimed, "Virginia is arrived!" and mistresses and servants embraced each other. Madame de la Tour said to Paul,--"My son, go and inform our neighbour of Virginia's arrival." Domingo immediately lighted a torch of bois de ronde, and he and Paul bent their way towards my dwelling.

It was about ten o'clock at night, and I was just going to extinguish my lamp, and retire to rest, when I perceived, through the palisades round my cottage, a light in the woods. Soon after, I heard the voice of Paul calling me. I instantly arose, and had hardly dressed myself, when Paul, almost beside himself, and panting for breath, sprang on my neck, crying,--"Come along, come along. Virginia is arrived. Let us go to the port; the vessel will anchor at break of day."

Scarcely had he uttered the words, when we set off. As we were passing through the woods of the Sloping Mountain, and were already on the road which leads from the Shaddock Grove to the port, I heard some one walking behind us. It proved to be a negro, and he was advancing with hasty steps. When he had reached us, I asked him whence he came, and whither he was going with such expedition. He answered, "I come from that part of the island called Golden Dust; and am sent to the port, to inform the governor that a ship from France has anchored under the Isle of Amber. She is firing guns of distress, for the sea is very rough." Having said this, the man left us, and pursued his journey without any further delay.

I then said to Paul,--"Let us go towards the quarter of the Golden Dust, and meet Virginia there. It is not more than three leagues from hence." We accordingly bent our course towards the northern part of the island. The heat was suffocating.

The moon had risen, and was surrounded by three large black circles. A fright-ful darkness shrouded the sky; but the frequent flashes of lightning discovered to us long rows of thick and gloomy clouds, hanging very low, and heaped together over the centre of the island, being driven in with great rapidity from the ocean, although not a breath of air was perceptible upon the land. As we walked along, we thought we heard peals of thunder; but, on listening more attentively, we perceived that it was the sound of cannon at a distance, repeated by the echoes. These omi-nous sounds, joined to the tempestuous aspect of the heavens, made me shudder. I had little doubt of their being signals of distress from a ship in danger. In about half an hour the firing ceased, and I found the silence still more appalling than the dismal sounds which had preceded it.

We hastened on without uttering a word, or daring to communicate to each other our mutual apprehensions. At midnight, by great exertion, we arrived at the sea shore, in that part of the island called Golden Dust. The billows were breaking against the bench with a horrible noise, covering the rocks and the strand with foam of a dazzling whiteness, blended with sparks of fire. By these phosphoric gleams we distinguished, notwithstanding the darkness, a number of fishing canoes, drawn up high upon the beach.

At the entrance of a wood, a short distance from us, we saw a fire, round which a party of the inhabitants were assembled. We repaired thither, in order to rest ourselves till the morning. While we were seated near the fire, one of the standers-by related, that late in the afternoon he had seen a vessel in the open sea, driven towards the island by the currents; that the night had hidden it from his view; and that two hours after sunset he had heard the firing of signal guns of distress, but that the surf was so high, that it was impossible to launch a boat to go off to her; that a short time after, he thought he perceived the glimmering of the watch-lights on board the vessel, which, he feared, by its having approached so near the coast, had steered between the main land and the little island of Amber, mistaking the latter for the Point of Endeavour, near which vessels pass in order to gain Port Louis; and that, if this were the case, which, however, he would not take upon himself to be certain of, the ship, he thought, was in very great danger. Another islander informed us, that he had frequently crossed the channel which separates the isle of Amber from the coast, and had sounded it, that the anchorage was very good, and that the ship would there lie as safely as in the best harbour. "I would stake all I am worth upon it," said he, "and if I were on board, I should sleep as sound as on shore." A third bystander declared that it was impossible for the ship to enter that channel, which was scarcely navigable for a boat. He was certain, he said, that he had seen the vessel at anchor beyond the isle of Amber; so that, if the wind rose in the morning, she would either put to sea, or gain the harbour. Other inhabitants gave different opinions upon this subject, which they continued to discuss in the usual desultory manner of the indolent Creoles. Paul and I observed a profound silence. We remained on this spot till break of day, but the weather was too hazy to admit of our distinguishing any object at sea, every thing being covered with fog. All we could descry to seaward was a dark cloud, which they told us was the isle of Amber, at the distance of a quarter of a league from the coast. On this gloomy day we could only discern the point of land on which we were standing, and the peaks of some inland mountains, which started out occasionally from the midst of the clouds that hung around them.

At about seven in the morning we heard the sound of drums in the woods: it announced the approach of the governor, Monsieur de la Bourdonnais, who soon after arrived on horseback, at the head of a detachment of soldiers armed with muskets, and a crowd of islanders and negroes. He drew up his soldiers upon the beach, and ordered them to make a general discharge. This was no sooner done, than we perceived a glimmering light upon the water which was instantly followed by the report of a cannon. We judged that the ship was at no great distance and all ran towards that part whence the light and sound proceeded. We now discerned through the fog the hull and yards of a large vessel. We were so near to her, that notwithstanding the tumult of the waves, we could distinctly hear the whistle of the boatswain, and the shouts of the sailors, who cried out three times, VIVE LE ROI! this being the cry of the French in extreme danger, as well as in exuberant joy;--as though they wished to call their princes to their aid, or to testify to him that they are prepared to lay down their lives in his service.

As soon as the Saint-Geran perceived that we were near enough to render her assistance, she continued to fire guns regularly at intervals of three minutes. Monsieur de la Bourdonnais caused great fires to be lighted at certain distances upon the strand, and sent to all the inhabitants of the neighbourhood, in search of provisions, planks, cables, and empty barrels. A number of people soon arrived, accompanied by their negroes loaded with provisions and cordage, which they had brought from the plantations of Golden Dust, from the district of La Flaque, and from the river of the Ram part. One of the most aged of these planters, approaching the governor, said to him,--"We have heard all night hollow noises in the mountain; in the woods, the leaves of the trees are shaken, although there is no wind; the sea-birds seek refuge upon the land: it is certain that all these signs announce a hurricane." "Well, my friends," answered the governor, "we are prepared for it, and no doubt the vessel is also."

Every thing, indeed, presaged the near approach of the hurricane. The centre of the clouds in the zenith was of a dismal black, while their skirts were tinged with a copper-coloured hue. The air resounded with the cries of the tropic-birds, petrels, frigate-birds, and innumerable other sea-fowl, which notwithstanding the obscurity of the atmosphere, were seen coming from every point of the horizon, to seek for shelter in the island.

Towards nine in the morning we heard in the direction of the ocean the most terrific noise, like the sound of thunder mingled with that of torrents rushing down the steeps of lofty mountains. A general cry was heard of, "There is the hurricane!" and the next moment a frightful gust of wind dispelled the fog which covered the isle of Amber and its channel. The Saint-Geran then presented herself to our view, her deck crowded with people, her yards and topmasts lowered down, and her flag half-mast high, moored by four cables at her bow and one at her stern. She had anchored between the isle of Amber and the main land, inside the chain of reefs which encircles the island, and which she had passed through in a place where no vessel had ever passed before. She presented her head to the waves that rolled in from the open sea, and as each billow rushed into the narrow strait where she lay, her bow lifted to such a degree as to show her keel; and at the same moment her stern, plunging into the water, disappeared altogether from our sight, as if it were swallowed up by the surges. In this position, driven by the winds and waves towards the shore, it was equally impossible for her to return by the passage through which she had made her way; or, by cutting her cables, to strand herself upon the beach, from which she was separated by sandbanks and reefs of rocks. Every billow which broke upon the coast advanced roaring to the bottom of the bay, throwing up heaps of shingle to the distance of fifty feet upon the land; then, rushing back, laid bare its sandy bed, from which it rolled immense stones, with a hoarse and dismal noise. The sea, swelled by the violence of the wind, rose higher every moment; and the whole channel between this island and the isle of Amber was soon one vast sheet of white foam, full of yawning pits of black and deep billows. Heaps of this foam, more than six feet high, were piled up at the bottom of the bay; and the winds which swept its surface carried masses of it over the steep sea-bank, scattering it upon the land to the distance of half a league. These innumerable white flakes, driven horizontally even to the very foot of the mountains, looked like snow issuing from the bosom of the ocean. The appearance of the horizon portended a lasting tempest; the sky and the water seemed blended together. Thick masses of clouds, of a frightful form, swept across the zenith with the swiftness of birds, while others appeared motionless as rocks. Not a single spot of blue sky could be discerned in the whole firmament; and a pale yellow gleam only lightened up all the objects of the earth, the sea, and the skies.

From the violent rolling of the ship, what we all dreaded happened at last. The cables which held her bow were torn away: she then swung to a single hawser, and was instantly dashed upon the rocks, at the distance of half a cable's length from the shore. A general cry of horror issued from the spectators. Paul rushed forward to throw himself into the sea, when, seizing him by the arm, "My son," I exclaimed, "would you perish?"--"Let me go to save her," he cried, "or let me die!" Seeing that despair had deprived him of reason, Domingo and I, in order to preserve him, fastened a long cord around his waist, and held it fast by the end. Paul then precipitated himself towards the Saint-Geran, now swimming, and now walking upon the rocks. Sometimes he had hopes of reaching the vessel, which the sea, by the reflux of its waves, had left almost dry, so that you could have walked round it on foot; but suddenly the billows, returning with fresh fury, shrouded it beneath mountains of water, which then lifted it upright upon its keel. The breakers at the same moment threw the unfortunate Paul far upon the beach, his legs bathed in blood, his bosom wounded, and himself half dead. The moment he had recovered the use of his senses, he arose, and returned with new ardour towards the vessel, the parts of which now yawned asunder from the violent strokes of the billows. The crew then, despairing of their safety, threw themselves in crowds into the sea, upon yards, planks, hen-coops, tables, and barrels. At this moment we beheld an object which wrung our hearts with grief and pity; a young lady appeared in the stern-gallery of the Saint-Geran, stretching out her arms towards him who was making so many efforts to join her. It was Virginia. She had discovered her lover by his intrepidity. The sight of this amiable girl, exposed to such horrible danger, filled us with unutterable despair. As for Virginia, with a firm and dignified mien, she waved her hand, as if bidding us an eternal farewell. All the sailors had flung themselves into the sea, except one, who still remained upon the deck, and who was naked, and strong as Hercules. This man approached Virginia with respect, and, kneeling at her feet, attempted to force her to throw off her clothes; but she repulsed him with modesty, and turned away her head. Then were heard redoubled cries from the spectators, "Save her!--save her!--do not leave her!" But at that moment a mountain billow, of enormous magnitude, ingulfed itself between the isle of Amber and the coast, and menaced the shattered vessel, towards which it rolled bellowing, with its black sides and foaming head. At this terrible sight the sailor flung himself into the sea; and Virginia, seeing death inevitable, crossed her hands upon her breast, and raising upwards her serene and beauteous eyes, seemed an angel prepared to take her flight to Heaven.

Oh, day of horror! Alas! every thing was swallowed up by the relentless billows. The surge threw some of the spectators, whom an impulse of humanity had prompted to advance towards Virginia, far upon the beach, and also the sailor who had endeavoured to save her life. This man, who had escaped from almost certain death, kneeling on the sand, exclaimed,--"Oh, my God! thou hast saved my life, but I would have given it willingly for that excellent young lady, who had persevered in not undressing herself as I had done." Domingo and I drew the unfortunate Paul to the ashore. He was senseless, and blood was flowing from his mouth and ears. The governor ordered him to be put into the hands of a surgeon, while we, on our part, wandered along the beach, in hopes that the sea would throw up the corpse of Virginia. But the wind having suddenly changed, as it frequently happens during hurricanes, our search was in vain; and we had the grief of thinking that we should not be able to bestow on this sweet and unfortunate girl the last sad duties. We retired from the spot overwhelmed with dismay, and our minds wholly occupied by one cruel loss, although numbers had perished in the wreck. Some of the spectators seemed tempted, from the fatal destiny of this virtuous girl, to doubt the existence of Providence: for there are in life such terrible, such unmerited evils, that even the hope of the wise is sometimes shaken.

In the meantime Paul, who began to recover his senses, was taken to a house in the neighbourhood, till he was in a fit state to be removed to his own home. Thither I bent my way with Domingo, to discharge the melancholy duty of preparing Virginia's mother and her friend for the disastrous event which had happened. When we had reached the entrance of the valley of the river of Fan-Palms, some negroes informed us that the sea had thrown up many pieces of the wreck in the opposite bay. We descended towards it and one of the first objects that struck my sight upon the beach was the corpse of Virginia. The body was half covered with sand, and preserved the attitude in which we had seen her perish. Her features were not sensibly changed, her eyes were closed, and her countenance was still serene; but the pale purple hues of death were blended on her cheek with the blush of virgin modesty. One of her hands was placed upon her clothes: and the other, which she held on her heart, was fast closed, and so stiffened, that it was with difficulty that I took from its grasp a small box. How great was my emotion when I saw that it contained the picture of Paul, which she had promised him never to part with while she lived! As for Domingo, he beat his breast, and pierced the air with his shrieks. With heavy hearts we then carried the body of Virginia to a fisherman's hut, and gave it in charge of some poor Malabar women, who carefully washed away the sand.

While they were employed in this melancholy office, we ascended the hill with trembling steps to the plantation. We found Madame de la Tour and Margaret at prayer; hourly expecting to have tidings from the ship. As soon as Madame de la Tour saw me coming, she eagerly cried,--"Where is my daughter--my dear daughter--my child?" My silence and my tears apprised her of her misfortune. She was instantly seized with a convulsive stopping of the breath and agonizing pains, and her voice was only heard in sighs and groans. Margaret cried, "Where is my son? I do not see my son!" and fainted. We ran to her assistance. In a short time she recovered, and being assured that Paul was safe, and under the care of the governor, she thought of nothing but of succouring her friend, who recovered from one fainting fit only to fall into another. Madame de la Tour passed the whole night in these cruel sufferings, and I became convinced that there was no sorrow like that of a mother. When she recovered her senses, she cast a fixed, unconscious look towards heaven. In vain her friend and myself pressed her hands in ours: in vain we called upon her by the most tender names; she appeared wholly insensible to these testimonials of our affection, and no sound issued from her oppressed bosom, but deep and hollow moans.

During the morning Paul was carried home in a palanquin. He had now recovered the use of his reason, but was unable to utter a word. His interview with his mother and Madame de la Tour, which I had dreaded, produced a better effect than all my cares. A ray of consolation gleamed on the countenances of the two unfortunate mothers. They pressed close to him, clasped him in their arms, and kissed him: their tears, which excess of anguish had till now dried up at the source, began to flow. Paul mixed his tears with theirs; and nature having thus found relief, a long stupor succeeded the convulsive pangs they had suffered, and afforded them a lethargic repose, which was in truth, like that of death.

Monsieur de la Bourdonnais sent to apprise me secretly that the corpse of Virginia had been borne to the town by his order, from whence it was to be transferred to the church of the Shaddock Grove. I immediately went down to Port Louis, where I found a multitude assembled from all parts of the island, in order to be present at the funeral solemnity, as if the isle had lost that which was nearest and dearest to it. The vessels in the harbour had their yards crossed, their flags half-mast, and fired guns at long intervals. A body of grenadiers led the funeral procession, with their muskets reversed, their muffled drums sending forth slow and dismal sounds. Dejection was depicted in the countenance of these warriors, who had so often braved death in battle without changing colour. Eight young ladies of considerable families of the island, dressed in white, and bearing palm-branches in their hands, carried the corpse of their amiable companion, which was covered with flowers. They were followed by a chorus of children, chanting hymns, and by the governor, his field officers, all the principal inhabitants of the island, and an immense crowd of people.

This imposing funeral solemnity had been ordered by the administration of the country, which was desirous of doing honour to the virtues of Virginia. But when the mournful procession arrived at the foot of this mountain, within sight of those cottages of which she had been so long an inmate and an ornament, diffusing happiness all around them, and which her loss had now filled with despair, the funeral pomp was interrupted, the hymns and anthems ceased, and the whole plain resounded with sighs and lamentations. Numbers of young girls ran from the neighbouring plantations, to touch the coffin of Virginia with their handkerchiefs, and with chaplets and crowns of flowers, invoking her as a saint. Mothers asked of heaven a child like Virginia; lovers, a heart as faithful; the poor, as tender a friend; and the slaves as kind a mistress.

When the procession had reached the place of interment, some negresses of Madagascar and Caffres of Mozambique placed a number of baskets of fruit around the corpse, and hung pieces of stuff upon the adjoining trees, according to the custom of their several countries. Some Indian women from Bengal also, and from the coast of Malabar, brought cages full of small birds, which they set at liberty upon her coffin. Thus deeply did the loss of this amiable being affect the natives of different countries, and thus was the ritual of various religions performed over the tomb of unfortunate virtue.

It became necessary to place guards round her grave, and to employ gentle force in removing some of the daughters of the neighbouring villagers, who endeavoured to throw themselves into it, saying that they had no longer any consolation to hope for in this world, and that nothing remained for them but to die with their benefactress.

On the western side of the church of the Shaddock Grove is a small copse of bamboos, where, in returning from mass with her mother and Margaret, Virginia loved to rest herself, seated by the side of him whom she then called her brother. This was the spot selected for her interment.

At his return from the funeral solemnity, Monsieur de la Bourdonnais came up here, followed by part of his numerous retinue. He offered Madame de la Tour and her friend all the assistance it was in his power to bestow. After briefly expressing his indignation at the conduct of her unnatural aunt, he advanced to Paul, and said every thing which he thought most likely to soothe and console him. "Heaven is my witness," said he, "that I wished to insure your happiness, and that of your family. My dear friend, you must go to France; I will obtain a commission for you, and during your absence I will take the same care of your mother as if she were my own." He then offered him his hand; but Paul drew away and turned his head aside, unable to bear his sight.

I remained for some time at the plantation of my unfortunate friends, that I might render to them and Paul those offices of friendship that were in my power, and which might alleviate, though they could not heal the wounds of calamity. At the end of three weeks Paul was able to walk; but his mind seemed to droop in proportion as his body gathered strength. He was insensible to every thing; his look was vacant; and when asked a question, he made no reply. Madame de la Tour, who was dying said to him often,--"My son, while I look at you, I think I see my dear Virginia." At the name of Virginia he shuddered, and hastened away from her, notwithstanding the entreaties of his mother, who begged him to come back to her friend. He used to go alone into the garden, and seat himself at the foot of Virginia's cocoa-tree, with his eyes fixed upon the fountain. The governor's surgeon, who had shown the most humane attention to Paul and the whole family, told us that in order to cure the deep melancholy which had taken possession of his mind, we must allow him to do whatever he pleased, without contradiction: this, he said, afforded the only chance of overcoming the silence in which he persevered.

I resolved to follow this advice. The first use which Paul made of his returning strength was to absent himself from the plantation. Being determined not to lose sight of him I set out immediately, and desired Domingo to take some provisions and accompany us. The young man's strength and spirits seemed renewed as he descended the mountain. He first took the road to the Shaddock Grove, and when he was near the church, in the Alley of Bamboos, he walked directly to the spot where he saw some earth fresh turned up; kneeling down there, and raising his eyes to heaven, he offered up a long prayer. This appeared to me a favourable symptom of the return of his reason; since this mark of confidence in the Supreme Being showed that his mind was beginning to resume its natural functions. Domingo and I, following his example, fell upon our knees, and mingled our prayers with his. When he arose, he bent his way, paying little attention to us, towards the northern part of the island. As I knew that he was not only ignorant of the spot where the body of Virginia had been deposited, but even of the fact that it had been recovered from the waves, I asked him why he had offered up his prayer at the foot of those bamboos. He answered,--"We have been there so often."

He continued his course until we reached the borders of the forest, when night came on. I set him the example of taking some nourishment, and prevailed on him to do the same; and we slept upon the grass, at the foot of a tree. The next day I thought he seemed disposed to retrace his steps; for, after having gazed a considerable time from the plain upon the church of the Shaddock Grove, with its long avenues of bamboos, he made a movement as if to return home; but suddenly plunging into the forest, he directed his course towards the north. I guessed what was his design, and I endeavoured, but in vain, to dissuade him from it. About noon we arrived at the quarter of Golden Dust. He rushed down to the sea-shore, opposite to the spot where the Saint-Geran had been wrecked. At the sight of the isle of Amber, and its channel, when smooth as a mirror, he exclaimed,--"Virginia! oh my dear Virginia!" and fell senseless. Domingo and I carried him into the woods, where we had some difficulty in recovering him. As soon as he regained his senses, he wished to return to the sea-shore; but we conjured him not to renew his own anguish and ours by such cruel remembrances, and he took another direction. During a whole week he sought every spot where he had once wandered with the companion of his childhood. He traced the path by which she had gone to intercede for the slave of the Black River. He gazed again upon the banks of the river of the Three Breasts, where she had rested herself when unable to walk further, and upon that part of the wood where they had lost their way. All the haunts, which recalled to his memory the anxieties, the sports, the repasts, the benevolence of her he loved,--the river of the Sloping Mountain, my house, the neighbouring cascade, the papaw tree she had planted, the grassy fields in which she loved to run, the openings of the forest where she used to sing, all in succession called forth his tears; and those very echoes which had so often resounded with their mutual shouts of joy, now repeated only these accents of despair,--"Virginia! oh, my dear Virginia!"

During this savage and wandering life, his eyes became sunk and hollow, his skin assumed a yellow tint, and his health rapidly declined. Convinced that our present sufferings are rendered more acute by the bitter recollection of bygone pleasures, and that the passions gather strength in solitude, I resolved to remove my unfortunate friend from those scenes which recalled the remembrance of his loss, and to lead him to a more busy part of the island. With this view, I conducted him to the inhabited part of the elevated quarter of Williams, which he had never visited, and where the busy pursuits of agriculture and commerce ever occasioned much bustle and variety. Numbers of carpenters were employed in hewing down and squaring trees, while others were sawing them into planks; carriages were continually passing and repassing on the roads; numerous herds of oxen and troops of horses were feeding on those wide-spread meadows, and the whole country was dotted with the dwellings of man. On some spots the elevation of the soil permitted the culture of many of the plants of Europe: the yellow ears of ripe corn waved upon the plains; strawberry plants grew in the openings of the woods, and the roads were bordered by hedges of rose-trees. The freshness of the air, too, giving tension to the nerves, was favourable to the health of Europeans. From those heights, situated near the middle of the island, and surrounded by extensive forests, neither the sea, nor Port Louis, nor the church of the Shaddock Grove, nor any other object associated with the remembrance of Virginia could de discerned. Even the mountains, which present various shapes on the side of Port Louis, appear from hence like a long promontory, in a straight and perpendicular line, from which arise lofty pyramids of rock, whose summits are enveloped in the clouds.

Conducting Paul to these scenes, I kept him continually in action, walking with him in rain and sunshine, by day and by night. I sometimes wandered with him into the depths of the forests, or led him over untilled grounds, hoping that change of scene and fatigue might divert his mind from its gloomy meditations. But the soul of a lover finds everywhere the traces of the beloved object. Night and day, the calm of solitude and the tumult of crowds, are to him the same; time itself, which casts the shade of oblivion over so many other remembrances, in vain would tear that tender and sacred recollection from the heart. The needle, when touched by the loadstone, however it may have been moved from its position, is no sooner left to repose, than it returns to the pole of its attraction. So, when I inquired of Paul, as we wandered amidst the plains of Williams,--"Where shall we now go?" he pointed to the north, and said, "Yonder are our mountains; let us return home."

I now saw that all the means I took to divert him from his melancholy were fruitless, and that no resource was left but an attempt to combat his passion by the arguments which reason suggested I answered him,--"Yes, there are the mountains where once dwelt your beloved Virginia; and here is the picture you gave her, and which she held, when dying, to her heart--that heart, which even in its last moments only beat for you." I then presented to Paul the little portrait which he had given to Virginia on the borders of the cocoa-tree fountain. At this sight a gloomy joy overspread his countenance. He eagerly seized the picture with his feeble hands, and held it to his lips. His oppressed bosom seemed ready to burst with emotion, and his eyes were filled with tears which had no power to flow.

"My son," said I, "listen to one who is your friend, who was the friend of Virginia, and who, in the bloom of your hopes, has often endeavoured to fortify your mind against the unforeseen accidents of life. What do you deplore with so much bitterness? Is it your own misfortunes, or those of Virginia, which affect you so deeply?

"Your own misfortunes are indeed severe. You have lost the most amiable of girls, who would have grown up to womanhood a pattern to her sex, one who sacrificed her own interests to yours: who preferred you to all that fortune could bestow, and considered you as the only recompense worthy of her virtues.

"But might not this very object, from whom you expected the purest happiness, have proved to you a source of the most cruel distress? She had returned poor and disinherited; all you could henceforth have partaken with her was your labour. Rendered more delicate by her education, and more courageous by her misfortunes, you might have beheld her every day sinking beneath her efforts to share and lighten your fatigues. Had she brought you children, they would only have served to increase her anxieties and your own, from the difficulty of sustaining at once your aged parents and your infant family.

"Very likely you will tell me that the governor would have helped you; but how do you know that in a colony where governors are so frequently changed, you would have had others like Monsieur de la Bourdonnais?--that one might not have been sent destitute of good feeling and of morality?--that your young wife, in order, to procure some miserable pittance, might not have been obliged to seek his favour? Had she been weak you would have been to be pitied; and if she had remained virtuous, you would have continued poor: forced even to consider yourself fortunate if, on account of the beauty and virtue of your wife, you had not to endure persecution from those who had promised you protection.

"It would have remained to you, you may say, to have enjoyed a pleasure independent of fortune,--that of protecting a loved being, who, in proportion to her own helplessness, had more attached herself to you. You may fancy that your pains and sufferings would have served to endear you to each other, and that your passion would have gathered strength from your mutual misfortunes. Undoubtedly virtuous love does find consolation even in such melancholy retrospects. But Virginia is no more; yet those persons still live, whom, next to yourself, she held most dear; her mother, and your own: your inconsolable affliction is bringing them both to the grave. Place your happiness, as she did hers, in affording them succour. My son, beneficence is the happiness of the virtuous: there is no greater or more certain enjoyment on the earth. Schemes of pleasure, repose, luxuries, wealth, and glory are not suited to man, weak, wandering, and transitory as he is. See how rapidly one step towards the acquisition of fortune has precipitated us all to the lowest abyss of misery! You were opposed to it, it is true; but who would not have thought that Virginia's voyage would terminate in her happiness and your own? an invitation from a rich and aged relation, the advice of a wise governor, the approbation of the whole colony, and the well-advised authority of her confessor, decided the lot of Virginia. Thus do we run to our ruin, deceived even by the prudence of those who watch over us: it would be better, no doubt, not to believe them, nor even to listen to the voice or lean on the hopes of a deceitful world. But all men,--those you see occupied in these plains, those who go abroad to seek their fortunes, and those in Europe who enjoy repose from the labours of others, are liable to reverses! not one is secure from losing, at some period, all that he most values,--greatness, wealth, wife, children, and friends. Most of these would have their sorrow increased by the remembrance of their own imprudence. But you have nothing with which you can reproach yourself. You have been faithful in your love. In the bloom of youth, by not departing from the dictates of nature, you evinced the wisdom of a sage. Your views were just, because they were pure, simple, and disinterested. You had, besides, on Virginia, sacred claims which nothing could countervail. You have lost her: but it is neither your own imprudence, nor your avarice, nor your false wisdom which has occasioned this misfortune, but the will of God, who had employed the passions of others to snatch from you the object of your love; God, from whom you derive everything, who knows what is most fitting for you, and whose wisdom has not left you any cause for the repentance and despair which succeed the calamities that are brought upon us by ourselves.

"Vainly, in your misfortunes, do you say to yourself, 'I have not deserved them.' Is it then the calamity of Virginia--her death and her present condition that you deplore? She has undergone the fate allotted to all,--to high birth, to beauty, and even to empires themselves. The life of man, with all his projects, may be compared to a tower, at whose summit is death. When your Virginia was born, she was condemned to die; happily for herself, she is released from life before losing her mother, or yours, or you; saved, thus from undergoing pangs worse than those of death itself.

"Learn then, my son, that death is a benefit to all men: it is the night of that restless day we call by the name of life. The diseases, the griefs, the vexations, and the fears, which perpetually embitter our life as long as we possess it, molest us no more in the sleep of death. If you inquire into the history of those men who appear to have been the happiest, you will find that they have bought their apparent felicity very dear; public consideration, perhaps, by domestic evils; fortune, by the loss of health; the rare happiness of being loved, by continual sacrifices; and often, at the expiration of a life devoted to the good of others, they see themselves surrounded only by false friends, and ungrateful relations. But Virginia was happy to her very last moment. When with us, she was happy in partaking of the gifts of nature; when far from us, she found enjoyment in the practice of virtue; and even at the terrible moment in which we saw her perish, she still had cause for self-gratulation. For, whether she cast her eyes on the assembled colony, made miserable by her expected loss, or on you, my son, who, with so much intrepidity, were endeavouring to save her, she must have seen how dear she was to all. Her mind was fortified against the future by the remembrance of her innocent life; and at that moment she received the reward which Heaven reserves for virtue,--a courage superior to danger. She met death with a serene countenance.

"My son! God gives all the trials of life to virtue, in order to show that virtue alone can support them, and even find in them happiness and glory. When he designs for it an illustrious reputation, he exhibits it on a wide theatre, and contending with death. Then does the courage of virtue shine forth as an example, and the misfortunes to which it has been exposed receive for ever, from posterity, the tribute of their tears. This is the immortal monument reserved for virtue in a world where every thing else passes away, and where the names, even of the greater number of kings themselves, are soon buried in eternal oblivion.

"Meanwhile Virginia still exists. My son, you see that every thing changes on this earth, but that nothing is ever lost. No art of man can annihilate the smallest particle of matter; can, then, that which has possessed reason, sensibility, affection, virtue, and religion be supposed capable of destruction, when the very elements with which it is clothed are imperishable? Ah! however happy Virginia may have been with us, she is now much more so. There is a God, my son; it is unnecessary for me to prove it to you, for the voice of all nature loudly proclaims it. The wickedness of mankind leads them to deny the existence of a Being, whose justice they fear. But your mind is fully convinced of his existence, while his works are ever before your eyes. Do you then believe that he would leave Virginia without recompense? Do you think that the same Power which inclosed her noble soul in a form so beautiful,--so like an emanation from itself, could not have saved her from the waves?--that he who has ordained the happiness of man here, by laws unknown to you, cannot prepare a still higher degree of felicity for Virginia by other laws, of which you are equally ignorant? Before we were born into this world, could we, do you imagine, even if we were capable of thinking at all, have formed any idea of our existence here? And now that we are in the middle of this gloomy and transitory life, can we foresee what is beyond the tomb, or in what manner we shall be emancipated from it? Does God, like man, need this little globe, the earth, as a theatre for the display of his intelligence and his goodness?--and can he only dispose of human life in the territory of death? There is not, in the entire ocean, a single drop of water which is not peopled with living beings appertaining to man: and does there exist nothing for him in the heavens above his head? What! is there no supreme intelligence, no divine goodness, except on this little spot where we are placed? In those innumerable glowing fires,--in those infinite fields of light which surround them, and which neither storms nor darkness can extinguish, is there nothing but empty space and an eternal void? If we, weak and ignorant as we are, might dare to assign limits to that Power from whom we have received every thing, we might possibly imagine that we were placed on the very confines of his empire, where life is perpetually struggling with death, and innocence for ever in danger from the power of tyranny!

"Somewhere, then, without doubt, there is another world, where virtue will receive its reward. Virginia is now happy. Ah! if from the abode of angels she could hold communication with you, she would tell you, as she did when she bade you her last adieus,--'O, Paul! life is but a scene of trial. I have been obedient to the laws of nature, love, and virtue. I crossed the seas to obey the will of my relations; I sacrificed wealth in order to keep my faith; and I preferred the loss of life to disobeying the dictates of modesty. Heaven found that I had fulfilled my duties, and has snatched me for ever from all the miseries I might have endured myself, and all I might have felt for the miseries of others. I am placed far above the reach of all human evils, and you pity me! I am become pure and unchangeable as a particle of light, and you would recall me to the darkness of human life! O, Paul! O, my beloved friend! recollect those days of happiness, when in the morning we felt the delightful sensations excited by the unfolding beauties of nature; when we seemed to rise with the sun to the peaks of those rocks, and then to spread with his rays over the bosom of the forests. We experienced a delight, the cause of which we could not comprehend. In the innocence of our desires, we wished to be all sight, to enjoy the rich colours of the early dawn; all smell, to taste a thousand perfumes at once; all hearing, to listen to the singing of our birds; and all heart, to be capable of gratitude for those mingled blessings. Now, at the source of the beauty whence flows all that is delightful upon earth, my soul intuitively sees, hears, touches, what before she could only be made sensible of through the medium of our weak organs. Ah! what language can describe these shores of eternal bliss, which I inhabit for ever! All that infinite power and heavenly goodness could create to console the unhappy: all that the friendship of numberless beings, exulting in the same felicity can impart, we enjoy in unmixed perfection. Support, then, the trial which is now allotted to you, that you may heighten the happiness of your Virginia by love which will know no termination,--by a union which will be eternal. There I will calm your regrets, I will wipe away your tears. Oh, my beloved friend! my youthful husband! raise your thoughts towards the infinite, to enable you to support the evils of a moment.'"

My own emotion choked my utterance. Paul, looking at me steadfastly, cried,--"She is no more! she is no more!" and a long fainting fit succeeded these words of woe. When restored to himself, he said, "Since death is good, and since Virginia is happy, I will die too, and be united to Virginia." Thus the motives of consolation I had offered, only served to nourish his despair. I was in the situation of a man who attempts to save a friend sinking in the midst of a flood, and who obstinately refuses to swim. Sorrow had completely overwhelmed his soul. Alas! the trials of early years prepare man for the afflictions of after-life; but Paul had never experienced any.

I took him back to his own dwelling, where I found his mother and Madame de la Tour in a state of increased languor and exhaustion, but Margaret seemed to droop the most. Lively characters, upon whom petty troubles have but little effect, sink the soonest under great calamities.

"O my good friend," said Margaret, "I thought last night I saw Virginia, dressed in white, in the midst of groves and delicious gardens. She said to me, 'I enjoy the most perfect happiness:' and then approaching Paul with a smiling air, she bore him away with her. While I was struggling to retain my son, I felt that I myself too was quitting the earth, and that I followed with inexpressible delight. I then wished to bid my friend farewell, when I saw that she was hastening after me, accompanied by Mary and Domingo. But the strangest circumstance remains yet to be told; Madame de la Tour has this very night had a dream exactly like mine in every possible respect."

"My dear friend," I replied, "nothing, I firmly believe, happens in this world without the permission of God. Future events, too, are sometimes revealed in dreams."

Madame de la Tour then related to me her dream which was exactly the same as Margaret's in every particular; and as I had never observed in either of these ladies any propensity to superstition, I was struck with the singular coincidence of their dreams, and I felt convinced that they would soon be realized. The belief that future events are sometimes revealed to us during sleep, is one that is widely diffused among the nations of the earth. The greatest men of antiquity have had faith in it; among whom may be mentioned Alexander the Great, Julius Caesar, the Scipios, the two Catos, and Brutus, none of whom were weak-minded persons. Both the Old and the New Testament furnish us with numerous instances of dreams that came to pass. As for myself, I need only, on this subject, appeal to my experience, as I have more than once had good reason to believe that superior intelligences, who interest themselves in our welfare, communicate with us in these visions of the night. Things which surpass the light of human reason cannot be proved by arguments derived from that reason; but still, if the mind of man is an image of that of God, since man can make known his will to the ends of the earth by secret mis sives, may not the Supreme Intelligence which governs the universe employ similar means to attain a like end? One friend consoles another by a letter, which, after passing through many kingdoms, and being in the hands of various individuals at enmity with each other, brings at last joy and hope to the breast of a single human being. May not in like manner the Sovereign Protector of innocence come in some secret way, to the help of a virtuous soul, which puts its trust in Him alone? Has He occasion to employ visible means to effect His purpose in this, whose ways are hidden in all His ordinary works?

Why should we doubt the evidence of dreams? for what is our life, occupied as it is with vain and fleeting imaginations, other than a prolonged vision of the night?

Whatever may be thought of this in general, on the present occasion the dreams of my friends were soon realized. Paul expired two months after the death of his Virginia, whose name dwelt on his lips in his expiring moments. About a week after the death of her son, Margaret saw her last hour approach with that serenity which virtue only can feel. She bade Madame de la Tour a most tender farewell, "in the certain hope," she said, "of a delightful and eternal re-union. Death is the greatest of blessings to us," added she, "and we ought to desire it. If life be a punishment, we should wish for its termination; if it be a trial, we should be thankful that it is short."

The governor took care of Domingo and Mary, who were no longer able to labour, and who survived their mistresses but a short time. As for poor Fidele, he pined to death, soon after he had lost his master.

I afforded an asylum in my dwelling to Madame de la Tour, who bore up under her calamities with incredible elevation of mind. She had endeavoured to console Paul and Margaret till their last moments, as if she herself had no misfortunes of her own to bear. When they were not more, she used to talk to me every day of them as of beloved friends, who were still living near her. She survived them however, but one month. Far from reproaching her aunt for the afflictions she had caused, her benign spirit prayed to God to pardon her, and to appease that remorse which we heard began to torment her, as soon as she had sent Virginia away with so much inhumanity.

Conscience, that certain punishment of the guilty, visited with all its terrors the mind of this unnatural relation. So great was her torment, that life and death became equally insupportable to her. Sometimes she reproached herself with the untimely fate of her lovely niece, and with the death of her mother, which had immediately followed it. At other times she congratulated herself for having repulsed far from her two wretched creatures, who, she said, had both dishonoured their family by their grovelling inclinations. Sometimes, at the sight of the many miserable objects with which Paris abounds, she would fly into a rage, and exclaim,--"Why are not these idle people sent off to the colonies?" As for the notions of humanity, virtue and religion, adopted by all nations, she said, they were only the inventions of their rulers, to serve political purposes. Then, flying all at once to the other extreme, she abandoned herself to superstitious terrors, which filled her with mortal fears. She would then give abundant alms to the wealthy ecclesiastics who governed her, beseeching them to appease the wrath of God by the sacrifice of her fortune,--as if the offering to Him of the wealth she had withheld from the miserable could please her Heavenly Father! In her imagination she often beheld fields of fire, with burning mountains, wherein hideous spectres wandered about, loudly calling on her by name. She threw herself at her confessor's feet, imagining every description of agony and torture; for Heaven--just Heaven, always sends to the cruel the most frightful views of religion and a future state.

Atheist, thus, and fanatic in turn, holding both life and death in equal horror, she lived on for several years. But what completed the torments of her miserable existence, was that very object to which she had sacrificed every natural affection. She was deeply annoyed at perceiving that her fortune must go, at her death, to relations whom she hated, and she determined to alienate as much of it as she could. They, however, taking advantage of her frequent attacks of low spirits, caused her to be secluded as a lunatic, and her affairs to be put into the hands of trustees. Her wealth, thus completed her ruin; and, as the possession of it had hardened her own heart, so did its anticipation corrupt the hearts of those who coveted it from her. At length she died; and, to crown her misery, she retained enough reason at last to be sensible that she was plundered and despised by the very persons whose opinions had been her rule of conduct during her whole life.

On the same spot, and at the foot of the same shrubs as his Virginia, was deposited the body of Paul; and round about them lie the remains of their tender mothers and their faithful servants. No marble marks the spot of their humble graves, no inscription records their virtues; but their memory is engraven upon the hearts of those whom they have befriended, in indelible characters. Their spirits have no need of the pomp, which they shunned during their life; but if they still take an interest in what passes upon earth, they no doubt love to wander beneath the roofs of these humble dwellings, inhabited by industrious virtue, to console poverty discontented with its lot, to cherish in the hearts of lovers the sacred flame of fidelity, and to inspire a taste for the blessings of nature, a love of honest labour, and a dread of the allurements of riches.

The voice of the people, which is often silent with regard to the monuments raised to kings, has given to some parts of this island names which will immortalize the loss of Virginia. Near the isle of Amber, in the midst of sandbanks, is a spot called The Pass of the Saint-Geran, from the name of the vessel which was there lost. The extremity of that point of land which you see yonder, three leagues off, half covered with water, and which the Saint-Geran could not double the night before the hurricane, is called the Cape of Misfortune; and before us, at the end of the valley, is the Bay of the Tomb, where Virginia was found buried in the sand; as if the waves had sought to restore her corpse to her family, that they might render it the last sad duties on those shores where so many years of her innocent life had been passed.

Joined thus in death, ye faithful lovers, who were so tenderly united! unfortunate mothers! beloved family! these woods which sheltered you with their foliage,--these fountains which flowed for you,--these hill-sides upon which you reposed, still deplore your loss! No one has since presumed to cultivate that desolate spot of land, or to rebuild those humble cottages. Your goats are become wild: your orchards are destroyed; your birds are all fled, and nothing is heard but the cry of the sparrow-hawk, as it skims in quest of prey around this rocky basin. As for myself, since I have ceased to behold you, I have felt friendless and alone, like a father bereft of his children, or a traveller who wanders by himself over the face of the earth.

Ending with these words, the good old man retired, bathed in tears; and my own, too, had flowed more than once during this melancholy recital.

The Codes Of Hammurabi And Moses
W. W. Davies

QTY

The discovery of the Hammurabi Code is one of the greatest achievements of archaeology, and is of paramount interest, not only to the student of the Bible, but also to all those interested in ancient history...

Religion   **ISBN:** *1-59462-338-4*   **Pages:132**
MSRP $12.95

The Theory of Moral Sentiments
Adam Smith

QTY

This work from 1749. contains original theories of conscience amd moral judgment and it is the foundation for systemof morals.

Philosophy **ISBN:** *1-59462-777-0*   **Pages:536**
MSRP $19.95

Jessica's First Prayer
Hesba Stretton

QTY

In a screened and secluded corner of one of the many railway-bridges which span the streets of London there could be seen a few years ago, from five o'clock every morning until half past eight, a tidily set-out coffee-stall, consisting of a trestle and board, upon which stood two large tin cans, with a small fire of charcoal burning under each so as to keep the coffee boiling during the early hours of the morning when the work-people were thronging into the city on their way to their daily toil...

Pages:84

Childrens   **ISBN:** *1-59462-373-2*   **MSRP $9.95**

My Life and Work
Henry Ford

QTY

Henry Ford revolutionized the world with his implementation of mass production for the Model T automobile. Gain valuable business insight into his life and work with his own auto-biography... "We have only started on our development of our country we have not as yet, with all our talk of wonderful progress, done more than scratch the surface. The progress has been wonderful enough but..."

Pages:300

Biographies/   **ISBN:** *1-59462-198-5*   **MSRP $21.95**

The Art of Cross-Examination
Francis Wellman

QTY

I presume it is the experience of every author, after his first book is published upon an important subject, to be almost overwhelmed with a wealth of ideas and illustrations which could readily have been included in his book, and which to his own mind, at least, seem to make a second edition inevitable. Such certainly was the case with me; and when the first edition had reached its sixth impression in five months, I rejoiced to learn that it seemed to my publishers that the book had met with a sufficiently favorable reception to justify a second and considerably enlarged edition. ..

Pages:412

Reference   ISBN: *1-59462-647-2*   *MSRP $19.95*

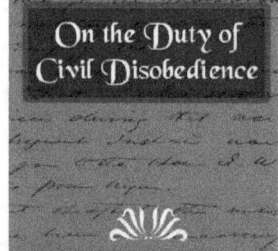

On the Duty of Civil Disobedience
Henry David Thoreau

QTY

Thoreau wrote his famous essay, On the Duty of Civil Disobedience, as a protest against an unjust but popular war and the immoral but popular institution of slave-owning. He did more than write—he declined to pay his taxes, and was hauled off to gaol in consequence. Who can say how much this refusal of his hastened the end of the war and of slavery?

Law   ISBN: *1-59462-747-9*   **Pages:48**

MSRP $7.45

Dream Psychology Psychoanalysis for Beginners
Sigmund Freud

QTY

Sigmund Freud, born Sigismund Schlomo Freud (May 6, 1856 - September 23, 1939), was a Jewish-Austrian neurologist and psychiatrist who co-founded the psychoanalytic school of psychology. Freud is best known for his theories of the unconscious mind, especially involving the mechanism of repression; his redefinition of sexual desire as mobile and directed towards a wide variety of objects; and his therapeutic techniques, especially his understanding of transference in the therapeutic relationship and the presumed value of dreams as sources of insight into unconscious desires.

Pages:196

Psychology   ISBN: *1-59462-905-6*   *MSRP $15.45*

The Miracle of Right Thought
Orison Swett Marden

QTY

Believe with all of your heart that you will do what you were made to do. When the mind has once formed the habit of holding cheerful, happy, prosperous pictures, it will not be easy to form the opposite habit. It does not matter how improbable or how far away this realization may see, or how dark the prospects may be, if we visualize them as best we can, as vividly as possible, hold tenaciously to them and vigorously struggle to attain them, they will gradually become actualized, realized in the life. But a desire, a longing without endeavor, a yearning abandoned or held indifferently will vanish without realization.

Pages:360

Self Help   ISBN: *1-59462-644-8*   *MSRP $25.45*

www.bookjungle.com *email: sales@bookjungle.com fax: 630-214-0564 mail: Book Jungle PO Box 2226 Champaign, IL 61825*

QTY

☐ **The Rosicrucian Cosmo-Conception Mystic Christianity** *by Max Heindel*　ISBN: *1-59462-188-8*　**$38.95**
The Rosicrucian Cosmo-conception is not dogmatic, neither does it appeal to any other authority than the reason of the student. It is: not controversial, but is: sent forth in the, hope that it may help to clear...　　　　New Age/Religion Pages 646

☐ **Abandonment To Divine Providence** *by Jean-Pierre de Caussade*　ISBN: *1-59462-228-0*　**$25.95**
"The Rev. Jean Pierre de Caussade was one of the most remarkable spiritual writers of the Society of Jesus in France in the 18th Century. His death took place at Toulouse in 1751. His works have gone through many editions and have been republished...　Inspirational/Religion Pages 400

☐ **Mental Chemistry** *by Charles Haanel*　ISBN: *1-59462-192-6*　**$23.95**
Mental Chemistry allows the change of material conditions by combining and appropriately utilizing the power of the mind. Much like applied chemistry creates something new and unique out of careful combinations of chemicals the mastery of mental chemistry...　New Age Pages 354

☐ **The Letters of Robert Browning and Elizabeth Barret Barrett 1845-1846 vol II**　ISBN: *1-59462-193-4*　**$35.95**
by Robert Browning and Elizabeth Barrett　　　　Biographies Pages 596

☐ **Gleanings In Genesis (volume I)** *by Arthur W. Pink*　ISBN: *1-59462-130-6*　**$27.45**
Appropriately has Genesis been termed "the seed plot of the Bible" for in it we have, in germ form, almost all of the great doctrines which are afterwards fully developed in the books of Scripture which follow...　Religion/Inspirational Pages 420

☐ **The Master Key** *by L. W. de Laurence*　ISBN: *1-59462-001-6*　**$30.95**
In no branch of human knowledge has there been a more lively increase of the spirit of research during the past few years than in the study of Psychology, Concentration and Mental Discipline. The requests for authentic lessons in Thought Control, Mental Discipline and...　New Age/Business Pages 422

☐ **The Lesser Key Of Solomon Goetia** *by L. W. de Laurence*　ISBN: *1-59462-092-X*　**$9.95**
This translation of the first book of the "Lernegton" which is now for the first time made accessible to students of Talismanic Magic was done, after careful collation and edition, from numerous Ancient Manuscripts in Hebrew, Latin, and French...　New Age/Occult Pages 92

☐ **Rubaiyat Of Omar Khayyam** *by Edward Fitzgerald*　ISBN: *1-59462-332-5*　**$13.95**
Edward Fitzgerald, whom the world has already learned, in spite of his own efforts to remain within the shadow of anonymity, to look upon as one of the rarest poets of the century, was born at Bredfield, in Suffolk, on the 31st of March, 1809. He was the third son of John Purcell...　Music Pages 172

☐ **Ancient Law** *by Henry Maine*　ISBN: *1-59462-128-4*　**$29.95**
The chief object of the following pages is to indicate some of the earliest ideas of mankind, as they are reflected in Ancient Law, and to point out the relation of those ideas to modern thought.　Religion/History Pages 452

☐ **Far-Away Stories** *by William J. Locke*　ISBN: *1-59462-129-2*　**$19.45**
"Good wine needs no bush, but a collection of mixed vintages does. And this book is just such a collection. Some of the stories I do not want to remain buried for ever in the museum files of dead magazine-numbers an author's not unpardonable vanity..."　Fiction Pages 272

☐ **Life of David Crockett** *by David Crockett*　ISBN: *1-59462-250-7*　**$27.45**
"Colonel David Crockett was one of the most remarkable men of the times in which he lived. Born in humble life, but gifted with a strong will, an indomitable courage, and unremitting perseverance...　Biographies/New Age Pages 424

☐ **Lip-Reading** *by Edward Nitchie*　ISBN: *1-59462-206-X*　**$25.95**
Edward B. Nitchie, founder of the New York School for the Hard of Hearing, now the Nitchie School of Lip-Reading, Inc, wrote "LIP-READING Principles and Practice". The development and perfecting of this meritorious work on lip-reading was an undertaking...　How-to Pages 400

☐ **A Handbook of Suggestive Therapeutics, Applied Hypnotism, Psychic Science**　ISBN: *1-59462-214-0*　**$24.95**
by Henry Munro　　　　Health/New Age/Health/Self-help Pages 376

☐ **A Doll's House: and Two Other Plays** *by Henrik Ibsen*　ISBN: *1-59462-112-8*　**$19.95**
Henrik Ibsen created this classic when in revolutionary 1848 Rome. Introducing some striking concepts in playwriting for the realist genre, this play has been studied the world over.　Fiction/Classics/Plays 308

☐ **The Light of Asia** *by sir Edwin Arnold*　ISBN: *1-59462-204-3*　**$13.95**
In this poetic masterpiece, Edwin Arnold describes the life and teachings of Buddha. The man who was to become known as Buddha to the world was born as Prince Gautama of India but he rejected the worldly riches and abandoned the reigns of power when...　Religion/History/Biographies Pages 170

☐ **The Complete Works of Guy de Maupassant** *by Guy de Maupassant*　ISBN: *1-59462-157-8*　**$16.95**
"For days and days, nights and nights, I had dreamed of that first kiss which was to consecrate our engagement, and I knew not on what spot I should put my lips..."　Fiction/Classics Pages 240

☐ **The Art of Cross-Examination** *by Francis L. Wellman*　ISBN: *1-59462-309-0*　**$26.95**
Written by a renowned trial lawyer, Wellman imparts his experience and uses case studies to explain how to use psychology to extract desired information through questioning.　How-to/Science/Reference Pages 408

☐ **Answered or Unanswered?** *by Louisa Vaughan*　ISBN: *1-59462-248-5*　**$10.95**
Miracles of Faith in China　　　　Religion Pages 112

☐ **The Edinburgh Lectures on Mental Science (1909)** *by Thomas*　ISBN: *1-59462-008-3*　**$11.95**
This book contains the substance of a course of lectures recently given by the writer in the Queen Street Hail, Edinburgh. Its purpose is to indicate the Natural Principles governing the relation between Mental Action and Material Conditions...　New Age/Psychology Pages 148

☐ **Ayesha** *by H. Rider Haggard*　ISBN: *1-59462-301-5*　**$24.95**
Verily and indeed it is the unexpected that happens! Probably if there was one person upon the earth from whom the Editor of this, and of a certain previous history, did not expect to hear again...　Classics Pages 380

☐ **Ayala's Angel** *by Anthony Trollope*　ISBN: *1-59462-352-X*　**$29.95**
The two girls were both pretty, but Lucy who was twenty-one who supposed to be simple and comparatively unattractive, whereas Ayala was credited, as her Bombwhat romantic name might show, with poetic charm and a taste for romance. Ayala when her father died was nineteen...　Fiction Pages 484

☐ **The American Commonwealth** *by James Bryce*　ISBN: *1-59462-286-8*　**$34.45**
An interpretation of American democratic political theory. It examines political mechanics and society from the perspective of Scotsman James Bryce　Politics Pages 572

☐ **Stories of the Pilgrims** *by Margaret P. Pumphrey*　ISBN: *1-59462-116-0*　**$17.95**
This book explores pilgrims religious oppression in England as well as their escape to Holland and eventual crossing to America on the Mayflower, and their early days in New England...　History Pages 268

QTY

The Fasting Cure *by Sinclair Upton*　　　　ISBN: *1-59462-222-1*　**$13.95**
In the Cosmopolitan Magazine for May, 1910, and in the Contemporary Review (London) for April, 1910, I published an article dealing with my experiences in fasting. I have written a great many magazine articles, but never one which attracted so much attention... New Age/Self Help/Health Pages 164

Hebrew Astrology *by Sepharial*　　　　ISBN: *1-59462-308-2*　**$13.45**
In these days of advanced thinking it is a matter of common observation that we have left many of the old landmarks behind and that we are now pressing forward to greater heights and to a wider horizon than that which represented the mind-content of our progenitors... Astrology Pages 144

Thought Vibration or The Law of Attraction in the Thought World　　ISBN: *1-59462-127-6*　**$12.95**
by William Walker Atkinson　　　　*Psychology/Religion Pages 144*

Optimism *by Helen Keller*　　　　ISBN: *1-59462-108-X*　**$15.95**
Helen Keller was blind, deaf, and mute since 19 months old, yet famously learned how to overcome these handicaps, communicate with the world, and spread her lectures promoting optimism. An inspiring read for everyone... Biographies/Inspirational Pages 84

Sara Crewe *by Frances Burnett*　　　　ISBN: *1-59462-360-0*　**$9.45**
In the first place, Miss Minchin lived in London. Her home was a large, dull, tall one, in a large, dull square, where all the houses were alike, and all the sparrows were alike, and where all the door-knockers made the same heavy sound... Childrens/Classic Pages 88

The Autobiography of Benjamin Franklin *by Benjamin Franklin*　　ISBN: *1-59462-135-7*　**$24.95**
The Autobiography of Benjamin Franklin has probably been more extensively read than any other American historical work, and no other book of its kind has had such ups and downs of fortune. Franklin lived for many years in England, where he was agent... Biographies/History Pages 332

Name	
Email	
Telephone	
Address	
City, State ZIP	

☐ **Credit Card**　　　☐ **Check / Money Order**

Credit Card Number	
Expiration Date	
Signature	

Please Mail to:　Book Jungle
PO Box 2226
Champaign, IL 61825
or Fax to:　　　630-214-0564

ORDERING INFORMATION

web*: www.bookjungle.com*
email*: sales@bookjungle.com*
fax*: 630-214-0564*
mail*: Book Jungle PO Box 2226 Champaign, IL 61825*
or PayPal *to sales@bookjungle.com*

Please contact us for bulk discounts

DIRECT-ORDER TERMS

20% Discount if You Order Two or More Books
Free Domestic Shipping!
Accepted: Master Card, Visa, Discover, American Express

www.ingramcontent.com/pod-product-compliance
Lightning Source LLC
Chambersburg PA
CBHW080835250626
47160CB00008B/2937